The Straight Man Reveals

The Straight Man Reveals

Christopher Trevor

Library of Congress Control Number:		2024907654
ISBN:	Softcover	979-8-3694-1974-8
	eBook	979-8-3694-1973-1

Print information available on the last page.

Rev. date: 04/10/2024

To order additional copies of this book, contact:
Xlibris
844-714-8691
www.Xlibris.com
Orders@Xlibris.com
859298

Contents

Author's Note ix

Annie doesn't live here anymore... 1
Vince Cole, his monster-sized nipples and Police Officers Ortiz and Burke.................... 9
Wesley Preston Learns His Lesson 18
Spanking the Groom on his, of all days, Wedding Day 29
A Soldier Tells His Story... 36
Paul's Nipples 42
Dominick.. 51
Nash 55
Archie and his Neighbor, Mr. Matthews 67
Archie and his Neighbor, Mr. Matthews 2 72
(Near?) Humiliating Experience 79
(Near?) Humiliating Experience (Chapter Two) 85
Mr. Thomas Vischel's Socks and Feet 90
Thanking Their Coach...96
Hotel Housekeeping 102
Jimmy, the Brutish Construction Worker (Do my dick) 108
Julian.. 111

Contents

This book is dedicated to my friend, Harris, who showed me all the reasons for not living my life in the closet. Rest in Peace, Harris…

Author's Note

AFTER I HAD TURNED 60 YEARS old this past July 3rd, my therapist said that when a person turns 60 that it's a good time to reflect back on the years of one's life.

At first I didn't think too hard about the doctor's statement, until I decided to have my newest book, "The Straight Man Reveals", published, because the subject matter of the stories in this book is indeed something, that for as long as I can remember, has intrigued me and on some level it has excited me as well, excited me in an erotic manner that is.

What I am referring to here are (supposedly) heterosexual men who have gay sexual experiences.

Although my book is a collection of fictional, erotic stories/fantasies, and even one story, which features a trans person (a first for me), as a starring character, I have, in my lifetime of 60 years now, known many supposedly straight men who had gay sexual experiences.

People who have read my past books know that many things, both unusual and very ordinary, have influenced me where my chosen genre is concerned.

Because of my love of so many styles of music, I pay tribute to that love with the story that leads the book off, a short harrowing story of a man in peril, something else that has fascinated me over the years of my life, called, "Annie Doesn't live here Anymore", which was obviously influenced by the song of the same name, and in my story things take a nasty turn for a young executive working at home during an average evening.

The story, "Vince Cole and the Nipple Chronicles", is a campy story where my lust for muscular men with big nipples and cops are concerned, when in the story an ordinary stop for driving over the speed limit leads to a sexy confrontation for the three stars of the tale.

Another huge erotic influence in my life that I have written about in various books of my short stories is man to man discipline/spanking. Because of that I have included two spanking tales for this book.

Men in uniform have been a constant fascination/obsession for me when it comes to my erotic fiction, and because of that I give you the story, "A Soldier tells his story."

Many of my readers over the years have told me how they love the two most villainous characters I have brought to life thus far, Cleeve and Otis, two notorious serial kidnappers of men. Cleeve and Otis have appeared in numerous collections of my short stories and they even had a starring role in my leather novel, "Love Torture and Redemption." Cleeve and Otis are back again in this book, in a story which could be the sister story to Vince Cole and the Nipple Chronicles, this Cleeve and Otis tale being titled, "Paul's Nipples."

The story titled, "Dominick", most definitely centers on the subject matter of this book and the story titled, "Nash" is homage to my Facebook friends who are into the erotic subject of gunge, something I feel that needs to have more attention paid to it.

The two chapters of the story titled, "Archie and his Neighbor", is first and foremost a story of a straight man having a most unexpected gay experience, but it is also a tribute to the TV series, Riverdale, Archie's character in this story being obviously loosely based on the character from Riverdale.

Just as with my two sinister characters, Cleeve and Otis, I don't feel that any collection of my short stories would be complete without an appearance made by my recurring character, tickle victim/hero, the gullible, loveable, always horny, married man, Timmy Backman. In this book Timmy Backman stars in a story titled, "Near Humiliating Experience."

The story, "Mr. Thomas Vischel's Socks and Feet", was influenced by a series of erotic pics I had come across on the wonderful website, http://Myfriendsfeet.com. This is the second story I have written where that website influenced my erotic imagination, the first being the story, Struggle, which appeared in my book of the same name.

In my story, "Thanking their Coach", I once more explore my unique and unusual passion for erotic superstitions in the world of sports.

Another favorite character of mine that I have brought to life in my fiction is superlative bank executive, the obscenely handsome, John Robinson. Mr. Robinson stars in my first ever transgender story, "Hotel Housekeeping." This story could actually be seen as an influence from the movie, "The Crying Game."

From as far back as I can recall sex in public has always been an erotic fascination for me. My story, "Jimmy, the Brutish Construction Worker", pays homage to this ever-loving fantasy setting for me, this time on a subway platform before the train barrels into the station.

The book is rounded out by the story, "Julian." This story was inspired by a Hispanic singer I met a few years ago at this point in my life-travels. Although this man is married to a woman and has children, I have always had the feeling that he would, under the right circumstances, venture into the world of gay experiences.

So with all this in mind, I welcome back my constant readers and also welcome any new readers of my work.

I thank you all for your support...

Christopher Trevor

Annie doesn't live here anymore

Inspired by the song,
Annie Doesn't Live Here Anymore.

IT WAS A SULTRY FRIDAY evening in mid-September, a Friday evening when most single, handsome young executives in their early thirties should be out after work, out on dates, out with their buddies, out in a bar enjoying an ice-cold beer and hobnobbing with the bartender. Or maybe just to be a little philosophical just be just out there, enjoying the pleasant weather.

But not Glenn Conway, who, on the third Friday night in a row was at home, sitting on his living room couch with a glass of white wine on the end table next to him and his laptop on his lap, as he worked on things he had once again brought home from work.

His navy blue calf-length nylon dress socks and white briefs told how he hadn't completely changed from the workday – gradually, his socks and briefs became his usual wear after work, while working from home. He propped up his feet on the coffee table in front of him and pecked away furiously at the laptop's keyboard.

"I really should have quit this rotten job. Screw this." Every thought piled more curses on his managers and encouraged him to type his resignation. *"I don't need this job. I can do so much better."* And his complacency soared as he hit the enter key harder every time.

Glancing up at the Howard Miller Lewis brand wall clock while taking a sip of wine, Glenn grumbled to himself, *"Damn Mr. Bradshaw for needing all this documentation. Who needs all this for a meeting? That goddamn 9:00 am Monday morning meeting! Third Friday night in a row, I haven't gotten to see Denise. I don't deserve this deprivation."*

The banking executive took another sip of his wine, set the glass back down on the end table, brought up the next document on his laptop, and resumed pecking away at the keyboard. *"I fucking need a better job."* While his hands worked tirelessly on the documents, his mind struggled with minimizing the flashbacks of his last night with Denise. *"Focus, you stupid brain of mine. I don't need this God-forsaken erection right now. I need to get this shit done."* A few more strict scolds and his mind steered back to the task at hand – getting the shit done.

By 9:00 pm, Glenn was glad to realize he was nearly done and figured he would send out for a late dinner of Japanese food.

"And have more wine," he chuckled to himself as he began sipping the third glass he had poured for himself, feeling relaxed and well-mellowed at that point. *"You're the only good thing tonight,"* he whispered to his half-empty glass and gulped down the remaining wine. As he set his wine glass down again on the end table, he heard the unmistakable sound of a key in a lock and the door to his luxury Manhattan apartment being opened.

"What the fuck?" Glenn said as fear gripped him momentarily. He quickly placed his laptop on the coffee table and got to his feet.

Thud. It was a clear thud, the door to his apartment slammed shut.

He slowly walked toward the kitchen, where the door to his apartment was. He thought of grabbing a knife on his way, but he quickly thought that it must be the building superintendent who had let himself into the apartment. Mike, the superintendent, had done that in the past when something needed fixing, but he always scheduled those things days in advance.

"Mike?" He merely moved his lips to say his name. He was expecting his rotund belly to make an appearance and his cap-covered head to become visible somewhere in the shadow. So Glenn dressed in his briefs and leftover dress socks from the workday didn't bother to put on more clothes. He waited, Mike typically didn't wait that long to make his presence known.

As he was about to call out, "Who's there?" Glenn heard a deep voice call, "Annie, Annie. Where are you?"

And then, Glenn saw a young dude with short cropped brown hair, dark sinister-looking eyes, dressed in jeans, a tee shirt, and heavy-duty, steel-toed mustard-colored construction boots. From the size of the stranger's arms, his biceps were the size of bowling balls. Glenn quickly figured he worked out eight hours or more every day of the week. And he knew he wouldn't choose to mess with this dude.

Seeing Glenn so scantily clad, the dude sneered, chuckled, and said, "Hey sexy boy. You're not Annie. Who are you?"

Feeling totally on display, Glenn felt that at least he needed to own the place he lived in and said, "I might just ask you the same thing."

"I'm Brad," the stranger said to Glenn, sounding ornery. "My girlfriend, Annie, lives here. I came to see her."

"Sorry dude, uh, Brad, Annie doesn't live here anymore," Glenn said as Brad took the big backpack he was carrying off his huge shoulders. "I moved in here like two months ago now."

"She didn't tell me she was moving," Brad said, sounding suddenly angry. "I mean what the fuck? I go away on business for a few weeks, and she up and moves?"

"And it would also appear the building owner didn't change the locks after I moved in," Glenn felt exposed and at risk, and said, "Annie obviously gave you a key, I see."

"Yeah, she did that," Brad said in a rather commandeering voice.

"Anyway, sorry but Annie doesn't live here anymore, and sorry about me not being properly dressed at the moment," Glenn began but Brad cut him off mid-sentence and said, "Come on man, fess up here, where's Annie?"

"I told you, she doesn't live here anymore, man," Glenn said, now sounding irritated. "Now look, I really want you to leave..."

"Why? So you can get back to fucking *my* girlfriend?" Brad asked, his voice rising in volume, "ANNIE!"

As he called out his girlfriend's name, Brad pushed Glenn sideways and stepped inside the bedroom. He stopped when he noticed a messed up bed and a pile of clothes on the chair. He knew Annie wouldn't live like this.

Stepping in front of the guy, Glenn said, "Look man, I told you. Annie doesn't live here anymore!"

"Yeah right, and you're just hanging out in your briefs and socks, sexy boy. I was born at night dude, but not last night," Brad barked, "NOW, get the fuck outa my way!"

But as Brad tried again to head to the bedroom, convinced to search the bedroom thoroughly, Glenn again stood in his way.

"Look man, I'm telling you, your girlfriend DOES NOT live here anymore!" Glenn repeated, "And I want you out of here. NOW!"

Reaching into his pocket, Brad brought out a set of keys. "If she doesn't live here then why do the keys that she gave me still open the door? DUDE, where's my fucking girlfriend?" Brad snapped, jingling the keys and tightening them in his fist, as he spoke.

"Fuck, I told you man, obviously the building owner didn't change the damned locks when I took over the apartment!" Glenn said his voice even louder now. "Now please, I'm feeling real on display here in just my damned briefs and socks and I don't want to ask you again to leave." Glenn pointed towards the door.

But this time, before he was able to complete his sentence, Brad stomped hard on his right, dress-socked foot, pressing it in hopes of squishing it completely.

"Oww! Holy shit, you son of a bitch!" Glenn cried out as he bent forward, wanting to free his foot. As he reached down to hoist his wounded foot up and massage it, Brad quickly stomped on the young executive's left, dress-socked foot.

"Oww! Fuck man! Those work boots of yours are vile!" Glenn reeled as he hopped stupidly around in agony. "Fucking fucks, gonna call the cops, you asshole!"

But as Glenn made to hobble to where he had hung his suit jacket over a chair earlier, to get his cell phone from its inside pocket, Brad quickly moved a few short feet in front of him and swiftly kicked Glenn in the balls.

Glenn let out a miserable sounding "OOOO!" and his hands instinctively moved over his crotch to protect it from any more attacks from the assailant who now had the drop on him. He involuntarily fell to his knees due to the pain in his stomped-upon feet.

"Awww! Shit!" Glenn moaned his hands over his wounded balls. The guy who had just entered his apartment now had him injured, reeling in pain and loomed threateningly and frighteningly over the young handsome executive.

Looking up at the guy, Glenn whimpered, through trembling lips, "G-get out of my apart…"

But before Glenn could complete his sentence, Brad reached down, grabbed the young executive by a handful of his hair, and with brute strength, hauled Glenn to his socked feet.

"Oww! Fuck! F-fuck you!" Glenn screamed as he was hauled upwards by his hair, bearing an indescribable pain.

As he trudged a bit on his wounded feet, Glenn said, "I-I'm telling you, man, *Annie doesn't live here.*"

But once again, Brad kicked him hard on his right ankle, and his steel-toed boots really delivered the impact.

"Oww!" Glenn howled in terrible pain and Brad then kicked the executive again, this time on his left ankle. "Ayy! Y-you're gonna break my goddamned feet, man!"

"Just want you a bit defenseless, sexy boy," Brad snickered, still holding onto the executive by the handful of his hair, and moved him toward the living room. He saw the glass of white wine on the end table and Glenn's laptop on the coffee table.

"Aw, looks like you were spending a nice relaxing evening all by yourself, huh sexy boy?" Brad tittered in Glenn's ear and yanked the poor young executive to his socked toes by the handful of his hair.

With his hands still placed over his aching balls, Glenn reeled, "Oww! Please, man, get out of my apartment! I've told you, your girlfriend, Annie, she doesn't live here anymore!"

"Yeah, so you've said," Brad said, a sadistic tone pronounced in his voice. And to Glenn's shock, the guy gave him a wet Bugs Bunny-style smooch on the cheek.

"But maybe *you* can be of some service to me, huh sexy boy?" Brad laughed and gave another wet smooch on Glenn's cheek.

Forgetting the pain in his balls and his socked feet, Glenn realized what the guy who had let himself into his apartment, now intended. He moved his hands away from his balls and began flailing his arms crazily, his fingers and thumbs clenched into meaty fists.

"Shit! Fuck you! *Service to you?*" Glenn reeled madly and clenched his teeth. "Fucking let go of me and get out." He managed to sound manlier than before and told himself not to whine like a girl.

But again, Glenn found himself careening forward, courtesy of Brad tossing him by his hair, across the coffee table, as he went knocking down his laptop with the top of his head.

As the laptop hit the living room floor, Glenn made a sound like "Uhhh!" and just like his laptop, he also fell to the floor from the top of the coffee table.

"Yuuhh!" The young executive moaned, thinking at that point that he was in a shit load of trouble here.

As his head spun from the blow it had just taken, and he squirmed on his stomach on the floor, Glenn heard Brad stomp toward him with his big booted feet.

Looking at Glenn's well-toned ass cheeks in his briefs, Brad grinned devilishly and said, "Oh, yeah sexy boy, you'll do just fine instead of Annie." He reached down, gripped Glenn's navy blue socked ankles in what felt to the guy like vise-like grips, and hoisted his feet a bit up. He began dragging him across the floor and toward the bedroom.

"Huh! Let, let go of my damned feet, man!" Glenn whimpered miserably as he was dragged along.

Hoisting the young executive's socked feet higher, Brad took a hearty sniff of them, moaned contentedly, and moved faster toward the bedroom with his captured cargo.

"Mmm, you got stinky socked feet, sexy boy. That just sent a charge to my barge. Ha!" Brad laughed meanly.

As Brad dragged him past the kitchen, Glenn looked glumly at where his suit jacket was, with his cell phone in its pocket, totally out of his reach, with no way of contacting help.

Then, before Glenn realized it, Brad had him in his bedroom.

"Nice, a queen-sized bed. Or is it a king-sized bed?" Brad said, took a deep breath, hoisted Glenn up by his socked feet into an upside-down position, and tossed the young executive onto the bed. Glenn felt like he was a helpless little girl being toyed around with by this mighty man.

"Fuck!" Glenn cried out, and the side of his head hit the wooden headboard, stunning him again. "Uhh!"

As he rolled over on the bed, his blurred vision revealed Brad stripping his clothes off, at what appeared to the young executive at lightning-like speed.

"Wh-what the fuck do you think you're doing?" Glenn mumbled in agony and shame.

Brad's vile chuckles grew louder, and he flung one of his heavy, steel-toed work boots directly at Glenn's forehead.

"Uhh!" Glenn bellowed his tongue stuck out of his mouth as the steel-toed section of the work boot hit his forehead, and he landed on his back on the bed, splayed out.

"Ha! Fucking bullseye!" Brad cackled and quickly got the rest of his clothing off. "Oh sexy boy, I'm beginning to thank the powers that be that Annie doesn't live here anymore, after all!"

Managing to hunch himself up on his elbows, Glenn saw the now totally naked Brad approaching the bed, his erect cock – *fuck that* – his erect, gigantic, thick, and long, what appeared to the young executive, even though his vision was still blurred, to be at least nine inches of tube steak.

"No, oh God no, not what am I thinking here?!" Glenn groaned in a mixture of misery and fear.

Brad mounted the bed, grabbed one of Glenn's upper arms, and in a hugely strong and fast motion, turned the executive over and onto his stomach, shouting down at him, "On your front section, sexy boy, I'm coming in for a landing here."

"No, no man, *please, no!*" Glenn pleaded and then felt his white briefs being torn and shucked off him. "Holy fucks man, I'm straight, and I'm not into what you're thinking here!"

"Aw man, yeah, sweet piece of ass you got here, sexy boy," Brad razzed, giving Glenn's coconut-shaped ass cheeks a few hard slaps with one hand, as he stroked his enormously erect cock with the other. "Your hole is gonna be just what my cock here needs tonight. Annie may not live here anymore, but I'm sure as fuck glad you do! And guess what? I'm straight too, but sometimes any port in a storm will do. Ha!"

With that, Brad stopped swatting Glenn's ass cheeks, let go of his erection, and pried the young executive's ass mounds wide apart, breathless then, as he said, "Aw, fuck, look at that sweet hole. Jeez, man, a fucking pink rosebud you got back here, sexy boy. Nice velvety-looking ass walls too. Fuck, thank GOD, Annie doesn't live here anymore!"

Then, Glenn heard the sounds of the guy who had overpowered him hacking up globs of saliva and phlegm, and he pried the young executive's ass globes further apart. Glenn cried out in pain, as Brad began spitting liberally into Glenn's anal canal.

"S-stop, stop this! Please stop this!" Glenn begged, gripping the bedsheets in his fists, his mind failing to make sense of what was happening to him.

"Look at that shit, sexy boy, your hole is sucking my homemade lube right in," Brad laughed, his erect cock now aimed directly at his target. "Your hole is meant for what I'm about to give it! So glad Annie doesn't live here anymore!"

And then, inch by painful inch to Glenn, Brad began inserting his huge, pre-cumming, erect as a flagpole cock into the hapless young executive's hole.

"AWWW! FUCK! No, no, you sick bastard!" Glenn reeled. "Dear God, you're deflowering me here, *ruining my asshole!*"

"More like a pussy hole you got back here, sexy boy," Brad grunted and slid his enormity further in, causing Glenn to feel his asshole being stretched beyond reason.

"Ohh God! Get it out, take it out of me, you sick fuck!" Glenn pleaded loudly. "My hole was never meant for this, oh, God!"

"You'll excuse me if I beg to differ, sexy boy," Brad jeered downward at his prize. "Your hole was *totally* meant for this!"

And with that, the guy who had shown up uninvited into his apartment slid his girth further yet into Glenn's hole – his moans synced with every inch he pushed further in.

"Aww gawd! What the fuck is wrong with you???" Glenn reeled, gripped the bedsheets tighter, and pressed his handsome face down into the sheets as well. "Please stop!"

But instead, Glenn felt Brad's cock break through his rosebud and his head snapped right back up from the bedsheets. Glenn felt as if something inside him had been torn away. A muscle, a tissue, or maybe his entire asshole had disintegrated.

"Arrh fucking fucks! You son of a bitch! You crazy bastard!" Glenn cried out then, as his assailant began thrusting in and out of his now very de-virgin-ized hole.

"Yeah, that's it sexy boy, talk dirty to me, curse me the fuck out! All that just drives me on all the more!" Brad chortled. "Just like Annie does when I fuck her good and hard."

And Brad did just that, or at least it felt that way to poor Glenn, as the guy seemed to be going deeper inside him with every pain-filled thrust.

"Fuck! Stop this and get the hell out! You sick moron!" Glenn ranted, although it sounded more like pleading at that point.

"Not for a while sexy boy, I got lots of staying power, that's why Annie loves me so much!" Brad laughed.

"Oh yeah? Then why did she move out of here and not let you know where she went?" Glenn thundered. In response, Brad increased his fucking motion, and the young executive realized he was being punished for his outburst.

"Arrhh! Goddamned bastard!" Glenn cried and buried his handsome face in the sheets. As Brad shot his load, slapping Glenn's ass cheeks hard at the same time, he grunted and swore like a marine who hadn't had sex in weeks, or maybe even months.

Glenn felt a mixture of physical pain, rage, and humiliation as the guy's warm sperm filled his hole and even seemed to overflow as he came and came like gangbusters.

After Brad finally shot his load into Glenn's hole, the young executive felt as if he had been brutally fucked for more than half an hour. Finally, when Brad was spent, he let his deflating cock slide slowly from his conquest's hole.

"Ahh, now that's what I would call a good fuck, sexy boy," Brad tittered. When his slimy cock was fully out of Glenn's hole, he gave the young executive some more hard swats on his ass.

"J-just please, please man; *just get the fuck out of here.*" Glenn pleaded again.

"Yeah, I suppose you're right, sexy boy. Annie doesn't live here anymore. Ha!" Brad laughed, and as he got himself dressed, Glenn lay on the bed whimpering over and over again, "Just get out of here."

When Brad was dressed, he stepped to the young executive's feet, swiped his blue dress socks off them, sniffed them real heartily a few times, and stuffed them in a pocket of his jeans, laughingly saying, "Seeing as I tore up your sexy briefs, I'll take your pretty socks here as a souvenir, sexy boy. Ha!"

"Y-you can have my goddamned socks, dude. Just please, get out of my apartment," Glenn said through his tears. He had never felt such humiliation before. He wanted to bury himself somewhere, knowing he wouldn't be able to face himself for a while, let alone Denise. In fact, Denise wasn't even the last of thoughts on his mind. He would take a long, long time to make sense of the last hour or so of his life.

Jingling his keys in Glenn's face, Brad mockingly said, "Be sure to tell the building owner to change that lock on your front door, sexy boy. Wouldn't want some dude getting in here, overpowering you, and using your asshole as if it were a pussy. *Ha!*"

And with that, Brad collected his backpack, headed to the door of the apartment, and left. A few minutes went by and as Glenn squirmed on his bed miserably, he asked himself, *"My God, what in all fucks just happened here?"*

He managed to get to his still aching, now bare feet, and as the pain in his balls seemed to have dissipated, he looked down at his nakedness and said stupidly to himself, *"Fucking bastard shredded my briefs and stole my socks. Fuck that, he stole more than my socks."*

The young executive hobbled to his dresser, and as he pulled a pair of gym shorts on, he next said to himself, *"Got to call the police before that fucking pervert gets too far."*

He got the gym shorts on, followed by a tee shirt, slipped his slippers onto his feet, and hobbled out of the bedroom toward the kitchen to get his cell phone from his suit jacket pocket. His asshole seemed to be burning.

It was when he'd reached the kitchen and rummaged his cell phone from the inside pocket that Glenn heard a knocking on the door to his apartment.

"Huh?" The young executive said, his hands suddenly shaking and ready to dial 911, thinking Brad had returned to visit more brutalities on him.

But then, after some more knocking, Glenn heard a female voice on the other side of the door, saying, "Hello, hello, is anyone home?"

"What the fuck?" Glenn whispered and slowly made his way to the door.

When he got there, he unlocked the door and slowly opened it. He saw a young lady, who he guessed was in her late twenties, blond, blue-eyed, and pretty, standing there with her hands gently resting on each other.

"C-can I help you?" Glenn asked the young lady, as she smiled at him. He didn't want any guests or any other person around him right now. He wanted to be alone and hoped desperately to get the pervert caught.

"Hi, I used to live in this apartment and I was wondering if maybe my boyfriend came by, looking for me. I've been out of town for a while and never gave him my new address," the young lady said to Glenn.

"My name is Annie."

/The End/

Vince Cole, his monster-sized nipples and Police Officers Ortiz and Burke...

SO THE WAY I HEARD IT, you want stories, *true stories*, about straight dudes who have had gay sexual experiences. Well, up until last week on Saturday when I was driving home from the gym after my usual morning workout, I was no longer a straight dude who'd never had any gay sexual experiences. Quite honestly, I thought straight dudes would rather be disgusted than tickled or aroused when touched – more like – fondled by another dude. Fuck, having gay sexual experiences was something I never even thought about until, as mentioned, last Saturday. I had accidentally gone a tad over the speed limit on the highway that I always use as a shortcut to get home. However, this time the damned air conditioning in my car had broken down, and I was sweating like a pig, and not to mention, *but* for the purposes of this narrative it needs to be mentioned, I was driving shirtless, something I don't usually do.

I mean, I wasn't looking to entice anybody – not any girl, let alone a dude. I'd never had any gay sexual experiences, but I have noticed gay dudes at the gym checking me out. I never did anything to try to entice them, and I wouldn't even tease them. To beat the heat of the day, I took off my shirt and rolled down the driver's side window. Still, I was suffering from the heat. I just wanted a nice cold shower; there was absolutely nothing else on my mind.

It was when I heard the sound of the police car's siren and saw the flashing lights on the top of the police car behind me, that the thought of a nice, cold shower seemed elusive. *"Fuck, fuck, fuck. What did I do?"* Clueless about the offense I made, however, convinced that something was wrong, I jeered loudly, *"Fuck! And now I have to stop on an open, hot as-hell lonely road. And I'm shirtless!"*

I brought my car to a stop and as I reached for my tee shirt lying on the passenger seat, I heard the cop approaching my car yell out, "Please place your hands on the steering wheel!" So with no choice in the matter, I quickly did as I was told.

The cop reached my car and stood a few inches from it, being able to fully see me in the car – Vince Cole, all muscular, pumped up, and shirtless. A part of me felt exposed and naked. I know police officers had way too many weird encounters, and seeing a shirtless guy didn't amount to the absurdities they may have witnessed. Still, I felt on display.

"Do you know why we pulled you over, sir?" the cop, who appeared to be Hispanic, asked me.

I glanced in my rearview mirror and saw his partner standing next to their cruiser on the passenger side.

"Uh, no Officer, I'm really not sure," I replied. *"Must be speeding."* There couldn't be any other offense, and I knew I was in a hurry to reach home.

"We clocked you going five to six miles over the speed limit," the Hispanic cop replied. "Could you please step slowly out of the car, sir?"

"Dang it. I knew it." I said, sounding regretful. Doing as the cop had said, keeping my hands in plain view, I opened the door of the car, stepped out, and said, "Was I really over the speed limit, officer? Well, I truly apologize. The air conditioning in my car is broken and I was trying to beat the heat and get home to my air-conditioned house."

Once I was standing in front of the cop, I saw him take in the sight of me or to be more precise, I saw him take in the sight of my robust and muscular chest or, to be even more precise, I saw him take in the sight of my hugely colossal, show-stopper-sized nipples.

"Oh yes, it has been a really hot summer," Officer Ortiz said and glared without shifting his eyes from my nipples. My mind was thinking of a hundred ways to cover myself, *"Maybe I could just ask him not to do this...this uncomfortable staring. Or just put my hands on my nipples? What if that offends him?"*

"Um, may I see your driver's license and registration, sir?" Officer Ortiz asked me, as I saw the name inscribed on his nameplate pinned to his dark blue uniform shirt.

"Of course, Officer," I said, and as I reached into the back pocket of my denim shorts, I saw the cop's hand move to his holstered weapon. At the same time, he gestured with his other hand for his partner to come over and join us.

As I handed Officer Ortiz my driver's license and car registration card, his partner sauntered closer to us. He was an Irish-looking dude, appearing to be in his late twenties to early thirties, and his nameplate read, 'Burke.'

When Officer Burke was standing next to Officer Ortiz, I saw how he instantly took in the sight of my humungous-sized nipples. But unlike Officer Ortiz, he didn't state a general fact or comment. He was amazed at the sight of my nebulous nubs as he licked his lips. *A few times.*

"Fuck, did he just lick his lower lip? I should have worn my shirt." I said to myself.

"What uh, what've we got here?" Burke asked Ortiz, attempting to act as professional as possible, struggling to keep his eyes off my nipples.

"Well, his license and registration check out, and he wasn't exceeding the speed limit by that much," Ortiz said and then looked at me, or, to be more precise, he stared at my giant nipples and then looked at my face. "Tell me, Mr. Cole, do you have any other priors you'd like to tell us about or should we run your license to find out?"

I smiled a half smile and replied, "Nope, no priors Officer Ortiz. And I assure you I'm telling you the gentleman's truth."

The two cops looked at each other and Ortiz said, "He told me the reason he was over the speed limit was because the air conditioning in his car was broken, and he was in a rush to get home to his air-conditioned house."

Office Burke looked at me and a snide expression came over his face. He licked his lips again and asked me, "That's why you were driving shirtless as well, Mr. Cole?" As he asked me that, I saw Officer Ortiz look at him quizzically because that wasn't a usual question for a cop to ask a man he's detained.

"Um, yeah, I suppose so, Officer Burke," I said. "But uh, is there a law against a man driving shirtless?"

"No, not really, but it works better in your defense to answer my question if you want to get off with just a warning for speeding, a smack of the wrist if you would," Burke replied and a bit of an authoritative tone had crept into his voice.

And lo and fucking behold, the man was stepping slowly closer to me. I could sense his raging desire, and for a moment, I felt myself being transfixed. I suppose this is how you feel when you are ashamed of your nakedness.

"Yeah, I'm guessing a warning will suffice in this case, Mr. Cole," Ortiz piped up, also stepping closer to me and handing me back my license and registration cards. *Does this count as an assault? What is happening?* I asked myself. I hoped I would have raised and voiced my objections, but my actions remained as composed as they ever were. I guess this is why silence can be deadly. *But was I even offended?*

As I reached with both my hands to place my wallet back into the pocket of my shorts, I saw the two cops stealing glances at my mountainous nipples. Of course, reaching for my back pocket caused my already mountainous nipples to jut out at the two officers.

"You were coming from the gym, Mr. Cole?" Officer Burke asked me, and I saw he furtively looked at my gym bag in the backseat.

"Uh, yes, sir," I said.

"Anything in that gym bag we might be interested in seeing?" Burke asked, sounding even more authoritative now.

"Well, only if you want to see my sweaty and smelly gym gear and my randy jockstrap," I replied with a grin.

And that's when it happened, something I never thought I would experience, and an immediate regret of being a sarcastic smart-ass.

Officer Burke was filled with anger, and fast as lightning, he grabbed my left-sided nipple with his thumb and first two fingers of one hand. Then he reeled in my face and said, "You getting sarcastic with me, Mr. Cole, Mr. Vince Cole? Is that it? You think all this is funny?" As he reeled, he squeezed down hard on my giant nub, twisting it hard as fuck at the same time.

"Oww! N-no, sir, Officer Burke, just stating what you would find in my gym bag if you were to search it. Oww, eas-easy with my nipple, Officer, please," I huffed in a mixture of pain and ecstasy, realizing in the backburner of my mind that I didn't do a thing to push the officer's hand off my nubs.

But instead of being easy with my nipple, the cop squeezed it harder, twisting it even faster at the same time. But this time, I cawed out a sound that sounded like, "Awwh," and Officer Ortiz proceeded to grab my right-sided nipple, squeezing it hard as fuck while his partner did the same to my other nipple. Both the cops twisted my beautiful nipples as if they were bottle caps.

"Arrhh. Please! Officers, stop. *Stop this please,*" I blathered crazily.

"We don't like people being sarcastic with us, Mr. Vince Cole!" Officer Ortiz barked directly into my ear, as he went on torturing the fucking fuck out of my right-sided nipple, and the tip of his tongue grazing my earlobe.

"I-I'm sorry, I do apologize, Officer Ortiz!" I pleaded.

My cock betrayed me by growing stiff and crusty; yep, I was turned on by two grown-ass men. *Men.* I never enjoyed a man's touch, fuck that, I never even remember a hug or a handshake from a man. I am a ladies' man. I cherish their curves, their ample bosom, and their curvy rumps. 'Voluptuous,' is what I call them – and is a word my ex-girlfriend taught me, other than many things she taught me. Darn it, my tent still gets pitched when I look at her photos – "those kinds of photos."

"But men? Do I even know myself?"

Frantically looking around, turning his head from side to side, Officer Ortiz then said, "There! Just up the road, a closed-down shack that used to be a shop of some sort!"

I looked around; searching for the spot, hoping someone else saw us.

Without a word, both cops let go of my oversized nipples, grabbed me by one upper arm each, and began moving me quickly toward the closed-down shack that used to be a shop of some kind, as said Officer Ortiz.

"WH-what goes on here, Officers?" I huffed cluelessly, my big nipples still smarting and tingling from the recent manhandling of them.

And fucking fucks of fucks, my nipple tips seemed to be leading the way to the closed-down shack along the road, and my hard as fuck cock wanted to release. This is not right. But at the same damned time, what's wrong with it?

"I'm straight. I'm fucking straight." My mind was screaming to me, but as I used to say, *"The cock wants what it wants,"* and then I wanted my climax.

"Fuck." I wanted to protest, but I protested silently.

When we reached the shack, Officer Burke kicked the door open with his tall booted foot and they half-dragged, half-walked me into the slightly cool, musty-smelling deserted business place.

In what seemed like no time, I found myself propped up against a post in between two aisles and my hands cuffed behind me and around the back of the post.

Officer Ortiz seemed to be running the show, the show starring my tremendous and jutted-up, hard nipples. Officer Burke enthusiastically played the supporting role. And I, well I, was the star and the audience enjoying the show.

"Fuck, fuck, fuck, never saw a pair of nipples like this before buddy!" Ortiz said to Burke, his voice trembling as he spoke.

"Look, Officers, this is going a bit beyond punishment for driving just a tad over the speed limit," I said pleadingly. "Don't you think?"

Neither of the cops responded to my plea and they continued with what they had begun out on the road by my car – fondling my nipples.

It's ironic how our perceptions change, even with things happening with us. It wasn't manhandling anymore. It was fondling now. Well, as far as my erect cock was concerned, it was a fucking good fondling.

Each of the cops grabbed one of my nipples each between their thumbs and first two fingers, squeezed and twisted the tar out of them.

"Awwh!" I cawed again. "Oh damn, my man tits, my poor man tits!"

Jeering in my ear, his tongue's tip flicked over my earlobe as he relentlessly squeezed and twisted my nipple, Officer Ortiz said, "Tell me Vince Cole, tell me, how did you manage to get your nipples so big, pointy, beefy, and hypnotically inviting?"

"Yeah, fucking tell us," Officer Burke said as he continued working the bejesus out of my other man-tit, "I mean, I'm married to a woman, a woman with awesome fucking tits at that, but never, never, have I seen a pair of nubs like yours and wanted to work 'em over like we're going to do to you here! Fuck, I never gave another dude's nipples a second thought. Until you that is Vince Cole. *Until you*. Fuck man, how'd you get your nipples so jumbo-sized?"

They then took my nipples by the center of them and as they squeezed them, they began trailing their fingers up and down as if they were masturbating my man tits – as if they were cocks on my chest.

"Rhee!" I railed crazily, arched my head a bit, and seethed, as what they were doing was sending icy shivers through my muscular being.

I stopped trying to make sense of what they were doing to me. I went with the flow, or more precisely, with the to-and-fro motion of their fingers.

"Fuck man, these fucking nipples, I can work them over all day bud," Officer Ortiz said to his partner.

"You and I both man, you and I both, follow my lead here. My wife loves it when I do this to her nipple tips." Burke said, and looked down again. I watched as he let go of my nipple that he was working on and pressed the pad of his index finger against the very tip of it. He then began rubbing it back and forth and in a swirling motion, as well.

I felt what I assumed was a mini-orgasm; any touch would now send tingles all across my body and after this, I mostly reached a point where I lost my some of my awareness.. ...something that, up until then, only women's bodies and touches had made happen for me.

"Okay man, do the same thing to his other nipple," Burke said to Ortiz. And the Hispanic cop didn't need to be told twice.

"Huhh! Oh, you fucking cops!" I moaned huskily. As indeed, what Burke did to his wife's nipples that she oh-so-loved, was proving to get the same reaction out of me.

The two officers rubbed and rubbed and swirled the tip of their index fingers over and over and over the very tips of my giant nubs, moving faster with each passing second to the point that they had me doing a stupid-looking dance in my sneakers as I leaned against the post I was handcuffed to.

"God! Faster! Harder!" I pressed my lips tight, not letting the stimulus my mind was sending, be let out verbally.

I couldn't encourage them more. They were already being relentless.

And as I did my stupid looking dance, the tent in my shorts was now at full mast and staining the front of my shorts with pre-cum. My nakedness didn't bother me, in fact, I wanted to rip away the only clothes covering me – *covering my manhood.*

When the very tips of my nipples felt numbed beyond reason, the two cops grabbed them meanly in their thumbs and index fingers and pulled on them, stretching the flesh as far as possible. Fucking fucks, it surged the ecstasy I was already feeling.

"Arrh!" I roared, my voice filling the closed-down shack we were in. I was grateful for this abandoned, located in the middle of nowhere, closed-down shack-cum-shop. Just a few minutes before, I was ashamed and felt on display, but that was a few minutes ago. A few minutes ago, when I was a strictly straight man. Now, I was moaning with the swirling rubs of my nubs by two men.

How little do we know ourselves? Ha, and I thought only women's sexual magic worked on me.

And as they went on stretching my nipple tips, Officer Burke again asked, "So tell us, Vince Cole, fucking tell us, how'd you get your nipples so jumbo-sized like they are? No man's nipples get like yours are on their own. What did you do to them? What did you feed these babies?"

As I was about to respond, both cops suddenly let go of my nipple tips, hunkered down a bit, and greedily and most unceremoniously gobbled my gigantic man nipples into their mouths. They instantly began sucking, slurping, chewing, and biting on them – to gratify their sexual hunger.

"Huh! Oh, my fucking gawd!! *Oh!*" I let out a needy moan at the suddenness of what the two cops were now subjecting my damned nipples to. "Fucking balls! My nipp...,"

I whimpered. Words became slippery for my tongue and mind, so I whimpered, only pleased 'hums' were let out of my mouth.

Next thing I knew, the two cops' heads were bobbing back and forth as they both got a good steady rhythm going. They continued working my nipples, sucking them, slurping crazily on them, dribbling their saliva profusely on them and sucking that saliva back heartily back into their craws, chewing and gnawing on the beef of them, driving me batty and battier, and especially into a tailwind when they swirled their tongues over my nipples in their mouths as if they were licking ice cream cones.

"Damn! Ahh!"

They pressed their tongues' tips against the very tips of my nipples and swirled those tongue tips round and round. They did everything possible to make me want more and more.

"Erhh!" I felt as if I would literally jump out of my sneakers and sweat socks.

"G-guys, Officee-rs," I huffed; my eyes squeezed shut and my erect cock churned in my shorts, "Plee-ase."

What was I pleading for? I didn't really know because the truth was, I was loving every blessed second of what the two crazy cops were doing to me – *to my nipples.*

And then of course came the climax.

The next thing I knew, after the two cops were furiously mouth-working my stupendously sized nipples, they reached down to my crotch and started teasing my cock and balls, squeezing and kneading them, God!

I arched my head back, clenched my teeth, and breathed raggedly as the two officers then worked the zipper down on my shorts, and then came the big reveal; my huge cock and testicles were on display, throbbing with desire.

Slurping sounds filled the area as the cops couldn't seem to get enough of mouth-working my nipples. Fuck, I wondered when they would stop and come up for air.

I didn't have much time to think at all, as my thoughts grew fuzzy when they used my pearly pre cum as a lube and took turns stroking my manhood, vying to see which of them would make me burst my load first.

I clenched my cuffed hands behind me into and out of fists. I trembled in my sneakers, and goosebumps broke out all over my well-muscled body. Fuck," as the two cops went on sucking my nipples, I felt as though I was somehow floating outside my body.

"I'll make you float outside your body" - it was something I told every woman I slept with. The roles now seemed to be reversed.

"Huh! It, it won't be long now, Officers," I said throatily, feeling my testicles churning and preparing to give up my load, "Uhh! Ohhh!"

And it was Officer Burke who would have won the prize – if they were giving away a prize for who had me in hand while I was masturbated.

"And thar he blows!" Officer Burke bellowed loudly when the first spurt of my mess erupted from my cock slit and splashed clear across the room.

"Awwh! Oh balls, *fucking balls!*" I railed crazily. It was beyond electric and astronomical, having my big nipples worked over and being made to cum at the same damned time.

"Amazing!" I thought but instead chose to say, "Fucking tit crazy cops you two are!"

My load spurted haphazardly all over the fucking place, and when I looked, I was shocked to see that it was now Officer Ortiz who had me in hand as I cummed like a madman.

Somehow, the cops had switched so that they would both get a chance at masturbating my load out of my balls. Well, after all, it wasn't just me having the pleasure.

When my load began dissipating, I was shivering to the point as if I were naked and outside in a snowstorm. I cummed some more, in response and approval to what the two cops were doing to my nipples - mouth-working them, hurting them but I loved every second of it.

For most guys, after they shoot a load, every part of them becomes sensitive to the touch, especially their nipples, that is, if those nipples are currently being sucked on like no one's business, while the said guy is shooting his load all over a closed-down shack on a lonely road, that used to be some sort of business. As mentioned before, I couldn't be more thankful for this abandoned shack.

Finally, when I was spent, Officer Burke, who had me in hand let go of my cock, and the two cops, seemingly reluctantly, stopped mouth-working my nipples.

"Are they done? Am I done? I think n.." Before I could complete that thought, I noticed their grins – and I knew what those grins meant. They licked their lips and ran their hands over the huge tents in their uniform pants.

Without a word, they both gobbled my sore as fuck giant nipples back into their mouths, began sucking them once more, and as they did so, they pulled the zippers down on their uniform pants and extracted their erect pre-cumming cocks from the fly openings.

While they worked my nipples, the two cops also managed to work each other's cocks. Officer Ortiz had Officer Burke's cock in hand and vice versa. *"What a kinky sight that was."*

As I huffed and gasped, the two cops sucked, chewed on, licked and this time, even kissed my nipples. It seemed that the sounds of ecstasy (maybe even the afterglow) I was making drove them all the more. They beat each other off faster and faster; the squishy sounds of men's cocks lubed with pre-cum and being masturbated filled the closed-down shack.

Amazingly, the two officers of the law shot their loads in unison, all over my sneakers and sweat socks. As they cummed, they didn't stop mouth-working my nipples for a second.

Officers Ortiz and Burke swore like marines who hadn't had sex in months as they breathlessly shot what seemed like days' worth of pent-up cop sperm. Once they were spent, they let go of each other's manhood and again, somewhat reluctantly, let my nipples slip out of their mouths.

"What a great way for a routine traffic stop to turn out," I said with a grin. I was wholly gratified. I don't think I had been masturbated this much for this long in months. Years, even.

As the two cops caught their breath and packed themselves back into their uniform pants, they both nodded in affirmation.

"I'll say this, Vince Cole," Officer Ortiz said, "You can thank your lucky stars you got tits better than a woman's there. If you didn't, I definitely would have ticketed you!"

At that, we all laughed raucously and it was Officer Burke who stepped behind the post to release me from the handcuffs.

As I stood there massaging my wrists, my semi-hard cock and testicles still on display outside my shorts, Officer Burke said, "So you never told us how you got your nipples to be so fucking oversized."

I chuckled a bit and said, "My wife loves big nipples. So after we got married, I worked on working them up to the way they are. It was a lot of time spent with alligator tit clamps snapped onto them, I used suction cups, both electronic and non-electronic, and over time my nipples were worked up nice and this big."

"Fuck, that's amazing. *Genius!*" Officer Ortiz said and as I proceeded to pack myself back into my shorts, the two cops gave my nipples a last kiss and suck each.

We exited the shack and as we walked back over to my car and the two officers' cruiser, we saw another cruiser and two cops standing there. When we'd reached my car, where the two new cops were standing, it was Officer Rusty, a handsome rookie-looking officer who said, "What goes on here? We've been radioing you two for the last half hour."

"Everything's under control, guys. We had a bit of a lesson to teach Mr. Vince Cole here for driving a bit over the speed limit earlier," Officer Ortiz chuckled, gesturing at my chest, or, to be more precise, he gestured at my robustly huge, sore and well-worked over nipples.

Officer Rusty and his partner, Officer Stanton, a cop who looked to be in his forties or so, took in the sight of my nipples, the cum all over my sneakers and sweat socks, looked at each other and just as Officers Ortiz and Burke had done, hustled me quickly back to the shack.

I didn't resist.

Shortly, back in the shack, I found myself again handcuffed to the post, as the two new cops went to work, or to be more precise, feasted heartily on my giant nipples.

/The End/

Wesley Preston Learns His Lesson

"Ow! Yow!"

Wesley Preston screamed out in pain as he lay over the older man's lap in the luxurious dining room, as the older man spanked and spanked and spanked, the thirty-three-year-old CEO's boxer briefs covered ass cheeks with a hand that was as strong as and the size of a bear's paw. "Ow! Dad, please!"

"I don't want to hear it, Wesley. I do not want to hear it! How a man your age is too old for an old-fashioned spanking," said Sydney Preston, Wesley's father — a stern older man with a powerful presence said, while bringing his huge hand down over and over and over again on his son's well-muscled upturned ass cheeks.

"Ow! Dad, please!" amidst the spanking, Wesley managed to protest, "I wasn't going to say that, Dad! Ow! God! I was just going to say it was a mistake. I made a silly damned mistake, an error in judgment, if you would. Ow!"

Ignoring his son's plea, Wesley's dad clenched his teeth, raised his paw-like hand high, and brought it crashing down, continuing to firmly spank Wesley's well-muscled left derriere, for at least twenty times, "Ouch!"

"Ay! Ow! Oh, for the love of God!" Wesley, clad only in tight white briefs and white sweat-soaked socks from his gym workout that night reeled and winced with each punishing blow as he dangled over his father's lap.

"Dad, please! It won't happen again! I'll be more careful next time I go to the gym!" Wesley pleaded, desperate for the spanking to stop.

But his father responded by spanking Wesley's other ass cheek just as firmly.

The sound of his father's huge hand connecting with and walloping his well-toned ass cheeks was maddening to the young executive. And the sting he was feeling meant that his father had already turned his pale white ass cheeks into a fiery red hue.

Wesley knew, rather felt, that this was only the beginning. He knew this because this was how it had always been! That trauma from his past he had, where his dad and the discipline his father meted out were concerned.

"How many times, Wesley?" the furious and fierce older man seethed as he continued to repeatedly spank his son's ass cheek. The sounds of *'Whap, Whap, Whap, Whap'* filling the luxurious dining room, "How many times have we been over this? Tell me, Wesley!"

Enraged, Wesley clenched his teeth and replied, "Enough times, Dad! Too many times! Far too many times, for God's sake, Dad!"

Sydney Preston yet again raised his hand and said, "Too many times. Exactly, son, *too many times*," and spanked the younger man's ass cheeks another forty times. "Too many times... *Too many damned times!*"

"AWWWWWWH! Dad, please, you never punished me so harshly before because of this!" Wesley cried now in anguish, his socked feet swinging behind him as his dad administered the series of forty swats.

"Your warm-up this time has to be longer than in the past, Wesley. I really have to make sure you've learned your lesson," the brutal older man said. "You think I like coming here to surprise my only son with a non-work visit and find you the way I found you?"

"No! No! I know you don't like finding me the way you found me, Dad, but," Wesley began to give his side of the explanation hoping his father would listen to his plea this time, but was again screaming in searing agony as his Dad scorched his ass cheeks some more. Each swat of the forty open-handed swats he was administering to his offspring was harder than the one before it. "AWWWWWHHHHH, Dad!" – Oh, the agony!"

"When you stopped at my office to say goodnight to me in your suit and tie and to tell me you were going to the gym, I didn't think for a second that the night would wind up with me having to tan and redden your buttocks, Wesley," Sydney Preston said sternly and walloped his son some more.

"Ow, Owwwwwwwww!" was the only thing Wesley could utter.

"Even though you are my son, you work for me too, in our company Wesley; you are the CEO of our company. And being the CEO and the owner's son, you have a responsibility to the poise and valiant image you project," the older man stated as he repeatedly stoked Wesley's ass cheeks.

"I know, Dad, I know. *I know!*" Wesley howled in pain and anger as his father continued the forty swats.

"Then why? When I came here to surprise you after your workout, why did I find you wearing white sweat socks, Wesley? Freaking white sweat socks are for teenagers! I've told you time and time *and time again!* Why don't you just understand?" the older man seethed and again and again spanked his son's ass mounds, the redness of them now showing through the thin white material of his briefs. The sounds of Wesley screaming and crying got louder and louder with each swat he received. "I've told you that even at the gym; you have an image to uphold! And I've told you that all corporate executives, especially the CEO, corporate executives wear black sweat socks. Black sweat socks, Wesley! With their gym gear!"

"Yes, Dad. Yes, I know. I forgot. I just forgot the damn protocol of being a CEO!" Wesley railed and punched the floor a few times.

"You forgot, you forgot, how could you forget Wesley?" The older man asked and swatted his son's ass cheeks some more, not tiring in the least, it seemed to the younger man. "I've spanked you for this countless times. Countless times, Wesley, *countless times!*"

As the sounds of '*Whap, Whap, Whap, Whap*' filled the air and the sting on his ass cheeks grew more and more intense, Wesley screamed out, "Dad, this is humiliating! What if Lucy was home? What if she wasn't away on a week-long business trip? Owwwwwwwww!"

"You think I wouldn't spank you in front of your wife, Wesley?" the older man asked and simply swatted his son's bottom twenty more times before he spoke again. "I would spank you in front of your wife. Hell, *I should* spank you in front of her, I should spank you in front of our board members, and I should spank you in front of your private office assistant!"

"Oh God, Dad! Oh God!" Wesley panted crazily. "All this over a damned pair of socks!"

"Yes, Wesley. All this over a damned pair of socks," the older man said.

After Sydney Preston swatted his son's ass twenty more times, he ordered his son to his feet, to his white sweat-socked feet, the damned white gym workout sweat socks he had been getting thrashed for!

Being the obedient son he was, *that he had always been*, Wesley did as he was told and stood there shaking in his socks and briefs, his hands over his face, his head hanging down, and crying like a five-year-old.

"Cry it out, Wesley. We will correct this ongoing problem yet, I promise you we will," Sydney Preston said, running a hand over his son's red as-a-tomato ass cheeks under his briefs. "Good warm-up, too, I must say. Your ass feels hot enough to fry an egg or two on."

After Wesley had cried for a good five minutes or so, his father said, "Look at me now, Wesley," and the younger man, *as always*, did as he was told.

"Y-yes, Dad?" Wesley whimpered, his tears soaking his face, his arms at his sides, his hands going nowhere near his ass to attempt to rub away the burn because he knew that if he did that there would be hell to pay.

"Now, Wesley, I want you to go into yours and Lucy's bathroom and come back with Lucy's wooden scrub-brush that she uses on her back," Wesley's Dad said, "We'll begin with that with your briefs off you."

Trembling now, Wesley snorted back a hank of snot. His tears flowed some more, and he pleadingly asked, "Dad, do we have to?"

In response, the unsparing father grabbed his son by his upper muscular arm, sat back down in the dining room chair, hauled his son back over his lap, and resumed swatting his ass with his huge bear paw-like hand.

"Owwwwwwwww, Owwwwwwww, Dad! No, no, Please!" Wesley begged.

"Looks like we're going to have two warm-ups this time, Wesley," the older man said, as he spanked his son's ass cheeks twenty more times. "And this is for having asked a stupid question!"

As the sounds of '*Whap, Whap, Whap*' again filled the room and his ass was fried again, Wesley's mind wandered back to how he had wound up in this humiliation for a man of his age and position, being spanked by his dear old dad.

It had been a long and crazy day at the Sydney Preston and Son Corporation. And even though Wesley didn't work out on Wednesdays, that day, after getting off from work, he figured a good intense workout before heading home would relieve the stress and anxiety he was feeling.

The handsome CEO always kept his gym bag ready with workout gear in his office, so it was no big deal to just go to the gym in the spur of the moment and being that his wife was out of town on a business trip and they had no kids there was nothing to worry about if he got home later than usual.

After pulling on his suit jacket, he looked through his gym bag to be sure he had everything he needed for a good hard work out.

"Damn, no sweat socks. Forgot to pack 'em after my last workout," Wesley said to himself, "No biggie. I'll buy a pair at the gym supply store they have in their lobby. No way am I going to work out in my dress socks, not after what Dad did to me last time he found out I did that. Jeez!"

He zipped his gym bag shut, hoisted it up by the handle, and left his office, closing and locking the door behind himself.

As he walked past his dad's office, which was two offices down the hall from his, he poked his head in the door and said, "Hey, Dad, heading out for the night."

"Good night, Wesley. Heading home?" Sydney Preston asked his son.

"Nah, not just yet. I'm going to hit the gym first," Wesley replied. "It was a crazy day. A good work out of lifting weights and some cardio mixed in will do me good."

"Okay, enjoy your workout then. Good night, son," the older Preston said. Wesley smiled, closed his father's office door, and headed to the elevators.

'*Working for his Dad wasn't the worst thing in the world*' was what Wesley Preston always said to himself. At least this way, he was guaranteed a job, and someday, when dear old Dad was gone, all of this would be his. *All of it!*

Those were the thoughts that were racing through the young man's mind as he descended in the elevator.

When he'd reached the lobby he walked over to the front desk security guard.

"Hey there, Will," Wesley said to the handsome, African American, uniformed security guard on duty that night at the desk.

"Hey, good evening, Mr. Preston," Will said, smiling wide at Wesley.

"Listen, I'm heading to the gym," Wesley said, "Please have a car there to pick me up around eight-thirty to take me home. I don't feel like having to change back into my suit and tie after I work out and take the train. I figure I'll just go straight home in a car after my work out."

"I'll take care of it, Mr. Preston," Will said.

"Thank you," Wesley replied and walked off and out of the building, unaware that the security guard was watching him go.

"Damn! What I wouldn't give to get me a piece of that handsome white boy's ass!" the security guard mused to himself, reached for his desk phone, and arranged for the town car to pick Wesley up from the gym at the time he had ordered.

When Wesley got to the gym, he showed his ID card to the pretty young lady at the front desk and proceeded to the gym's supply store, which was a few steps down from the front desk, unaware that the pretty young receptionist was watching him go.

"Damn, what a shame he's married," she said to herself, "I would give anything to get with Mr. Wesley Preston. He is so charming."

In the gym supply store, Wesley walked up to the front counter where two hunky, well-built trainers were manning the place.

"Good evening, Mr. Preston," the blond trainer said as Wesley stepped up to the counter. "How can we help you tonight?"

"I need sweat socks, please," Wesley replied. "I have everything else I need gear-wise, but I forgot to pack sweat socks, and I don't want to work out in my dress socks. That would look silly."

"Yes sir, sweat socks it is," the blond trainer said, reached under the counter, and produced a pair of white calf length sweat socks. "Twelve dollars, Mr. Preston or you could just have me charge it to your monthly dues?"

"Yeah, uh, do that, uh, Frank," Wesley said looking at the young trainer's nametag pinned to his gym uniform tee shirt. "You uh, you don't have any black sweat socks?"

"Sorry, Mr. Preston," the dark-haired trainer behind the counter, his nametag reading Norman, said, "We just sold the last pair."

"Yeah," Wesley said, unsure for a moment what to do.

"Fuck it," he then said to himself, "my dad will never know."

Little did he know...

He took the sweat socks and headed to the locker room to change out of his office suit and tie and to his gym gear.

After he was gone from the gym supply store, Norman said to Frank, "Damn, what I could do to that handsome suit!"

"You and I both bud," Frank chuckled. "You and I both!"

Wesley dashed down to the locker room, changed out of his suit and tie and to his gym gear, and quickly emerged a few minutes later upstairs in the state-of-the-art gym.

The handsome and young CEO worked out with weights and cardio machines and even took a Pilates class.

When he arrived home at nearly nine o'clock that night, Wesley Preston was stress-free and felt very invigorated yet pleasantly exhausted.

"Have a good night, Mr. Preston," the driver of the town car said as he opened the door for Wesley, and the young man emerged, still wearing his black gym shorts, a white tee-shirt, white sneakers, and the white sweat socks he had purchased a few hours earlier at the gym supply store.

"You too, Seth," Wesley said to the driver as he walked toward the front door of the luxury apartment building he lived in with his beautiful wife, Lucy.

As the chauffeur uniformed driver watched Wesley walking toward his apartment building, he said to himself, "Damn, if his father knew what I wanted to do to him. That ass, my God, that well-muscled, perfect ass!"

The doorman of the building held the door open for Wesley as he entered. He, like all the others before him, entertaining lust-filled thoughts where the handsome CEO was concerned, said, "Good evening" to Wesley, wished him a good night, and watched him walk toward the elevator bank.

Wesley took the elevator to the top floor of the building and walked on his sneaker-clad feet to his apartment, figuring he would have a light dinner of a mixed salad with some grilled chicken on top or maybe a soup, then take a shower and get to sleep.

But as he unlocked the door to his apartment, the young man had no idea just how his evening would turn out.

He closed and locked the door behind himself, dropped his gym bag to the floor, and proceeded first to the luxurious bathroom so he could take a much-needed shower. It was as he stripped off his tee shirt, took off his sneakers, and shucked his gym shorts off that he heard the front door to the apartment opening and then being closed and locked.

"What the hell?" Wesley said out loud, as he stepped from the bathroom in just his tight white briefs and calf-length white sweat socks. "Lucy, is that you?"

But when Wesley stepped into the living room and saw his dad standing there, the young man's heart sank like the Titanic. Seemed like he was struck by lightning. Poor Wesley.

"Dad..." Wesley said.

"I thought I would surprise you, and we would have dinner together after your work out," Sydney Preston said, holding up a key. "I used the key you and Lucy gave me."

But as he spoke, the smile that was on Sydney Preston's face slowly disappeared as he took in the sight of those dreaded white sweat socks his son was wearing.

"But it looks like it's you who has surprised me again. *Again, Wesley!*" the older man reeled, stripping off his suit jacket and tossing it ragingly on the couch.

"Dad, listen, please. *Please listen,* I had forgotten to pack black sweat socks. Black sweat socks that I do have here. You can check my sock drawer," Wesley began justifying as his dad stepped to the dining room, Wesley following him without even having to be told to do so. "When I got to the gym, I went to their supply store to buy black sweat socks for my work out, but they were sold out. All they had were these white ones I'm wearing now."

Wesley watched miserably as his dad pulled a dining room chair to the corner of the spacious eating area and sat down.

"And I did remember what you did to me last time I forgot black sweat socks and worked out in my OTC black silks." Wesley went on but was suddenly silenced as his Dad was pointing at his lap.

The handsome young CEO swallowed hard before he found his voice again.

"Oh, come on, Dad, really? *Do we have to?*" Wesley pleaded.

"You don't have to, Wesley. *I have to!*" Sydney Preston seethed and pointed at his lap again. "I believe you know the drill, Wesley."

"Y-yes, Dad, I do..." Wesley stated and, without another word, positioned himself over his dad's lap like a little kid who had misbehaved.

Now, Wesley's mind snapped back to the present, as his dad was giving his much-reddened ass cheeks a second warm-up that evening. The CEO squirmed, writhed, seethed, and punched the floor as his muscular ass-globes were whapped and spanked hard to a fiery shade of crimson.

As Wesley screamed and cried, his dad asked him, "Tell me, Wesley. What will you do the next time I order you to bring me a spanking implement, such as Lucy's scrub brush?" Sydney Preston asked his son.

"I'll bring it to you, Dad! I won't question your orders again!" Wesley heaved. "My God, two warm-ups!"

"Two warm-ups indeed, Wesley. Two indeed," Sydney Preston said as he raised his hand high and repeatedly brought it crashing down hard on his son's behind. "Tell me why you're getting a second warm-up this time out, Wesley. *Tell me!*"

Before his son could speak, Sydney Preston swatted the younger man's ass cheeks ten hard times.

"BE-because I asked a stupid question, Dad!" Wesley responded through his tears and through the wads of snot that were streaming from his nose and landing on the floor in front of him. "I'm getting a second warm-up because I asked a really stupid question! Yowwwwwwwww!"

As Wesley responded to his dad's question, the older man swatted and whapped and again, swatted, then whapped his upturned ass cheeks more and more.

Finally, to Wesley's relief, the second warm-up of having his ass spanked that evening didn't last as long as the first one had, but there was still more coming. The CEO knew his Dad too well where discipline was concerned, especially discipline where the littlest details in life were concerned; details that don't even matter, insignificant minor details that might not make a difference to any normal human being, but Sydney Preston? He was far from normal!

"On your feet again, Wesley, or should I say, on your white sweat-socked feet," Wesley's Dad ordered. Shaking, trembling and crying like crazy, the CEO did as he was told.

Standing there once more with his hands over his handsome face and sobbing, Wesley muttered, "Two warm-ups, my God, two warm-ups. My ass feels like it's on fire, Dad."

"And whose fault is it that we had to have two warm-ups this evening, Wesley?" Sydney Preston asked his son.

"Mine, Dad. No one's fault but mine," Wesley sobbed into his hands.

As his Father looked him over, he said, "White sweat socks, dress your feet like a teenager's, and you'll receive the discipline a teenager receives."

Slowly, Wesley moved his hands away from his face, placed his arms at his sides, and said, "Yes, Dad, you're correct. You're correct as always…" and sniveled back a huge hank of snot.

"Now, Wesley, to the bathroom with you and bring back your wife's scrub brush that she uses on her back," Wesley's dad said for the second time that evening.

"Yes, Dad," Wesley said and started walking toward the bathroom, his reddened ass cheeks stinging horribly with each step he took on his white sweat-socked feet, the reason for his being spanked this evening.

"Oh, and Wesley," Sydney Preston called out.

Wesley turned, looked at his Dad, and said, "Yes, Dad?"

"Be sure to come back not only with Lucy's scrub brush but be sure you're de-under-panted as well," the older man snickered.

Without responding, Wesley turned and proceeded to the bathroom, filled with utter and total humiliation.

In the bathroom, he quickly took off his white briefs, dropped them in the hamper, reached into the tub, and took his wife's scrub brush from the shower caddy where she kept it hanging.

"Fucking thirty-three years old, and my Dad spanks me, fucking thirty-three years old," Wesley said to himself as he looked at the scrub-brush, *"Fuck…"*

The CEO stepped over to the toilet, opened the lid, stood over it, and pissed long, hard and frothy, his cock shriveled and his testicles tucked under it as if in fear.

A few scant moments later, Wesley emerged from the bathroom holding the scrub brush he had been ordered to get, wearing just the white sweat socks that had gotten him into the spanking predicament he was in now.

When he saw his father gesturing toward him with a finger to hurry up, Wesley hung his head in shame, sauntered quickly over to the older man, and handed him the wooden scrub brush.

Even though he had been in the gym's locker room naked and with his private parts on total display, it always made him feel all the more humiliated to be that way in front of his dad.

In what seemed like seconds, Wesley Preston found himself back over his dad's lap and wailing yet again.

"Yowwwwwwww! Owwwwwwwww! Oh God, Dad!" the CEO was opera-singing, it seemed as his dad walloped his now naked red ass cheeks with the backend of his wife's scrub brush.

"Ah, if only Lucy knew what this brush was used for when she's not here, eh Wesley?" Sydney Preston asked his handsome offspring.

"Ayyyyy, yeah. If she only knew!" Wesley reeled, punched the floor, and endured twenty more hard swats on his left ass cheek from the wooden scrub brush, then twenty hard swats on his right ass cheek, then twenty hard swats on both his ass cheeks.

"Dad, please! Yowwwwwwwwwwww!" Wesley screamed crazily now.

"We're going for eggplant purple this time, Wesley," the older man said, raising the scrub brush and bringing it down first hard, then harder, and then the hardest, on his son's naked ass cheeks.

Wesley was able to feel the welts sprouting and his skin literally twitching as his Dad did his work with the scrub brush.

"Owwwwwwww!" Wesley yowled more and more, clenched his hands into fists, and pressed his knuckles against the floor.

"Tell me what I want to hear, Wesley, tell me what I want to hear, and we'll be done here tonight," Sydney Preston said.

But before Wesley could speak, the older man *'Whapped, Whapped, Whapped and Whapped'* his son's behind over and over again with the wooden scrub brush. Wesley screamed and cried and figured his dad wasn't kidding when he said they were going for eggplant purple this evening where the color of his ass cheeks was concerned.

"Tell me, Wesley. *Tell me!*" Sydney Preston said and whapped his son's ass some more.

"I-I'll never, I'll never wear... Ow! I'll never wear white sweat socks to the gym for my work out again. Never again!" Wesley screamed insanely, "Please, Dad. Please stop now!"

"Good man, Wesley, good man," the older man said and stopped whapping his son's behind with the scrub brush.

Sydney Preston sat there with his son over his lap, Wesley crying profusely as the older man rubbed the palm of his hand over and over the younger man's eggplant-purpled welted ass cheeks.

"I think this time out we've really solved the problem, Wesley," Sydney Preston said, dropping the scrub brush to the floor.

"Y-yes, Dad. Yes, we did... You did, I mean... You solved the problem for me," Wesley sniveled as he lay still over his Father's lap. "No more white sweat socks for me... *No more...* When I learned that they didn't have any black sweat socks to sell at the gym's supply store, I should have just not worked out at all."

"Good man, Wesley, good and better judgment. Now, on your feet," Wesley's Father said, and the handsome but in pain CEO climbed slowly off his father's lap.

"Weep, young man," the older man said, and he also got to his feet.

"Yes, Dad," Wesley said, crossed his hands up behind his head, looked down at the floor, and cried and cried and cried. In fact, he sobbed, sniveled, and cried. Then cried a little more...

"And tell me again what I want to hear," Sydney Preston said.

As he cried, sobbed, trembled in his white sweat socks, and looked down at the floor, and as his ass cheeks stung and twitched like the devil, Wesley Preston said, "I will never wear white sweat socks to the gym for my work out ever again."

"Very good, Wesley, very good," Sydney Preston said. "Now, go to your bedroom, put on a proper pair of gym shorts, a tee shirt, and black sweat socks. While you do that, I'll call downstairs and have your doorman have some dinner sent up for us from that Chinese place nearby that we both like."

"Yes, Dad," Wesley said, putting his arms around his dad, hugging him tight, and even though he hadn't showered yet, he proceeded to his bedroom to do as his dad had ordered him, as he always did where obeying his dad was concerned.

Sydney Preston hugged his son tight, gave his purple ass a gentle squeeze, and said, "Go get properly dressed, Wesley. I'll call downstairs."

"Yes, Dad," Wesley said and scampered quickly to his and his wife's bedroom.

A short while later, Wesley emerged from the bedroom wearing a pair of black gym shorts, a white tee shirt, and calf-length black sweat socks.

"Now, isn't that better, Wesley?" Sydney Preston asked his son as he stepped into the dining room.

"Yes, Dad, much better," Wesley said agreeably but sounding oh-so-miserable at the same time. "Can I uh, have a pillow to sit on while we eat?"

Wesley's Dad chuckled and said, "I suppose that's permissible. Oh, and the food is on the way."

"Okay, good, I am hungry after all; what with the workout I put myself through at the gym and then you spanking me. I guess all that really gave me an appetite," Wesley said, trying to smile.

"Yes, one would think so, Wesley," the older man said, looking down at his son's feet. "Wear black sweat socks to the gym from now on and your ass won't suffer the consequences."

"Right you are, Dad," Wesley said, "I'll uh, go and get that pillow."

Wesley once more went to his and his wife's bedroom to get a pillow to sit on while he and his Dad had their dinner.

It was fifteen minutes later when the phone rang.

"I got it, Dad," Wesley said, picking up the phone, knowing from the caller ID display that it was Luke, the doorman. "Hello? Hi Luke, yes, please send him up. Thanks."

Wesley put the phone down and said to his dad, "I'll pay for it, Dad."

"No bother, Wesley, I already put it on your charge card," the older man said, grinning from ear to ear. "And Mr. Wang himself, the owner, is delivering our dinner."

Upon hearing those words, Wesley swallowed hard and asked his father, "Mr. Wang, *Mr. Wang* himself is coming here, Dad?"

"Yes, he's on his way up now," Sydney Preston said and glanced at the scrub brush that was still on the floor where he had left it earlier.

"Oh, crap! Oh, crap! *Oh, fucking crap!*" Wesley whispered, shaking in his black sweat socks now.

A few minutes later, the buzzer to Wesley's apartment sounded, and his dad said, "Answer the door, Wesley."

"Dad, really?" Wesley said, "I swear to you, I've learned my lesson."

"I said answer the door, Wesley," the older man repeated.

Wesley took a deep breath, walked to the door of his apartment, opened it, and saw the owner of the Chinese restaurant he usually frequented standing there.

"Good evening, Mr. Wang. Won't you come in, Sir?" Wesley asked as the older Chinese gentleman walked past him with a large shopping bag filled with his and his dad's delicious dinner.

Mr. Wang said hello to Wesley's Father. The two older men shook hands, and then Mr. Wang picked up the scrub brush.

"Your father tells me you wore white sweat socks to the gym tonight, Wesley!" the Chinese restaurant owner shouted as he sat down in the same chair that Sydney Preston had sat in earlier.

A few moments later, Wesley was over the Chinese man's lap, his gym shorts and briefs pulled down in the back, and his purple ass was being even further purpled now.

"Owwwwwwwww! Owwwwwwwww! Yowwwwwwwwwwwwwww!" Wesley screamed as Mr. Wang pummeled his ass cheeks, and his father sat

Spanking the Groom on his, of all days, Wedding Day

"HERE'S TO YOU, DAD," newly married man, Cory Andrews, proclaimed in front of his family, friends, co-workers, and other guests during his wedding reception, as he raised a flute of champagne to his dear father. "Thanks for all the ass whippings you gave me throughout the years. It's because of you that I am the man I am. Thanks for all the lessons you taught me, through tough discipline."

With that, amid some reluctant-sounding applause, Cory sipped from his flute, and a few moments later, the guests joined in and raised their glasses to toast the newlyweds.

Grinning happily, Cory returned to his seat at the dais and sat back down next to his beautiful young wife, Kathleen.

After the handsome groom had taken another sip of his champagne, Kathleen turned to him with a look of uncertainty on her face.

"What's wrong, babe?" Cory inquired, curious about his wife's expression.

"Um, I have to say I am quite taken aback. I cannot believe the toast you just made to your dad," Kathleen interjected. "And uh, he whipped your ass while you were growing up?"

"He sure did. Dad knew how to keep me in line," Cory responded. "Although whipping was Dad's word for it. It was actually more like he paddled me. He would use his old fraternity paddle from college most times, but when he felt I really needed a lesson, he would bring out the black round leather paddle, and boy, howdy did that leather device really cook my ass."

"Y-you never told me about that," Cory's wife said, sounding very confused. "Your dad used to paddle you, and you never told me?"

"Well, I suppose it was a thing between me and my dad, but I felt it was appropriate to express my gratitude to him today, on yours and my special day," Cory explained, "I would say my toast conveyed respect and humility."

Gulping down a sip of her champagne, Kathleen asked, "And how old were you when your dad stopped, uh, paddling you, as you just put it?"

"He hasn't stopped," Cory admitted, "The last time my Dad paddled me was the morning after my bachelor party. I mean, as I had told you, I had totally behaved at the bachelor party, but dad just wanted to paddle me as a reminder to always behave myself, especially as a married man."

With a look of astonishment on her face, Kathleen said, "Your dad paddled you the morning after your bachelor party? Cory that was last weekend. *You can't be serious!*"

"Yeah, I know, that's just Dad's way, you know!" Cory replied, smiling and nodding at some of the wedding guests walking past the dais.

"So, um, now that we're married, your father won't paddle you anymore, right?" Kathleen asked.

"I really don't know, babe," he said.

"*You don't know?*" Kathleen asked in disbelief.

"Well, I mean, it's up to him," Cory said, sounding totally reasonable.

"Cory, you're married now, *we're married now*," Kathleen went on. "And you're a grown man. You're too old for your Dad to still be paddling you. God!"

"Heh, yeah, right, tell my Dad that." Cory chuckled and gulped down the last of his champagne.

Not believing what her husband just told her, Kathleen tried to process it, but the next question that abruptly popped out of her mouth was, "So you're saying that your dad is going to come to our house and paddle you?"

Looking at Kathleen in disbelief now, Cory said, "No, no way will my dad come to our house and paddle me."

"Oh, okay," Kathleen sighed in relief.

"He'll have me come over to his and my stepmom's house and paddle me in my old room," Cory said, and this time, Kathleen's jaw dropped. She couldn't believe her ears.

When the wait staff began serving the main course, Cory said, "I'm going to go and use the restroom in the groom's lounge, babe. Dad always said I had to wash my hands before eating. If I didn't, he would paddle me till my butt shined like the sun."

This time, Kathleen did not respond; it was all too overwhelming for her to absorb what her husband had just told her. She simply watched as her husband dashed away from the dais, but the thoughts that went through her head were that she had known Cory for two years, had been engaged to him for the second year, and not once had he told her that his father still paddled him, or worse, that he *allowed* his father to still paddle him.

As Kathleen sat at the dais with thoughts jumbling up in her mind of her husband's dad paddling him, Cory made his way down the long corridor toward the groom's lounge.

He entered and quickly made a beeline into the restroom and up to a urinal. As he stood relieving himself, he heard the door to the groom's lounge open and close again.

"Heh! Seems like someone else needs to drain the vein as well," Cory chuckled and said to himself. "Of course, I told Kathleen I needed to wash my hands. Dad taught me never to announce I had to relieve myself. My goodness, if I did that, he would paddle me till my butt shined like the top of the Chrysler building, as he always stated it."

Shortly, when Cory was done urinating, and no one had come in to use the restroom with him, he packed himself back into his tuxedo pants, zipped up, thoroughly washed his hands, and exited the bathroom.

When he emerged into the lounge he saw his two ushers, Joe and Mike, standing in the center of the lavish and luxurious room. Curiously, they were both standing with their hands placed behind their backs.

"Hey guys, no need to wait. The bathroom has various urinals and stalls," Cory said, smiling at his two ushers.

Grinning devilishly, Mike, a muscle-bound guy who made his living as a personal trainer in a gym, said, "We didn't come in here to use the restroom, Cory."

"No?" Cory asked. "Then why did you come in here? Need to get away from all the noise for a bit? I wish I could too, but you see, I am the groom, heh!" said Cory, winking at both the ushers.

Grinning equally as devilishly, Joe, another stack of muscles who made his living as a construction worker, piped up, "Let's just say your toast to your dad was totally over the top and coincidental."

"Well, I was just being honest," Cory replied. "My dad always kept me on the straight and narrow when he would...uh...when he...would..."

But then, Cory's jubilant mood and his joyful-sounding rhetoric ceased when he saw his two ushers moving their hands from behind their backs and that they were each holding a round leather paddle.

"Um, guys, what, uh, what's this all about?" Cory asked, looking at his two ushers now with total trepidation.

"Let's just say your dad asked us to help make sure you continue to stay in line, Cory," Mike said and winked evilly at the handsome groom.

"C-continue to stay in line?" Cory asked.

"Yeah, now that you're married, that is," Joe said, holding up his paddle.

"But guys, it's my wedding day," Cory said through quivering lips.

"Your Dad told us you'd say that, how you always seemed to have an excuse to avoid being paddled, but he said to tell you there's no better day than a man's wedding day to redden his behind," Mike replied to the shocked groom.

Standing there feeling dumbfounded, Cory said, "Yeah, my dad would actually say something like that. Where uh, where did you two get the leather paddles? They look like exact replicas of the one my dad uses to paddle me with."

As the two ushers took small steps toward Cory, Joe said, "Unbeknownst to you, your dad gave them to us at the end of your bachelor party. He said to think of them as very special party favors."

"My dad planned to have you two paddle me here at my wedding? I can't believe this." Cory asked, not backing away from the two ushers, his heart racing and his cock churning in his tuxedo pants, the reaction he always had when he knew his dad was about to paddle him red. The groom called it becoming fear hard.

When Joe and Mike were standing mere inches from Cory, the handsome groom said, "I still cannot believe that my dad would have me paddled on my wedding day and by two of my ushers at that. I mean, I remember him having our next-day neighbor paddle me, and my Uncle Angelo sometimes paddled me, but two ushers at my wedding? No, no, no. *I can't believe it...*"

"Heh! You got to believe it, Cory boy," Mike said and tweaked the groom's bowtie. "Now then, tuxedo pants and briefs down around your knees... HEH... it's time for your wedding day paddling..." and the next thing Cory knew, he was undoing his tuxedo pants. He never disobeyed when it came to being paddled, *never.*

Then, Joe was seated on a lounge couch, and the groom found himself over his usher's lap, with his tuxedo pants mortifyingly pulled down in the back, along with his frosty white briefs, the way he had been instructed to do, and his exquisitely shaped, well-muscled white as snow ass sticking straight up, a bulls-eye for the two ushers' paddles...

Just as when his Dad would paddle him, it all seemed to happen so fast when he landed across the man's lap. But then, Cory's thoughts were cut short when Joe raised his paddle, and the dreaded sounds of *'Whap, Whap, Whap, Whap, Whap'* filled the area.

"Ow, oh Jeez, oh God! Ow!" Cory bellowed, not just at the pain but at the suddenness of it. "Fuck! Holy shit, you guys, I'm really being paddled at my own wedding!" Cory was startled.

As Joe whapped Cory's ass over and over, he tauntingly said to the groom, "Of course, you're really being paddled at your own wedding. Did you think we would disobey your Dad? We wouldn't even think of it."

'Whap, Whap, Whap, Whap, Whap,' went Joe's leather paddle as it stung and kissed Cory's ass.

"N-no, c-can't, O-owwwwwwwww!" Cory squealed then. "Can't disobey my Dad! Won't disobey my Dad! Never disobey my Dad! *Damn!"*

'Whap, Whap, Whap, Whap, Whap'

After what felt like close to 60-70 swats, Joe stopped paddling Cory's ass.

As he gently rubbed the paddle over the groom's white, turned to a shade of pink ass, Joey said, in a devilish tone of voice, "Good start!"

"Good start? Jeez Louise..." Cory said and, within less than a few moments, found himself splayed across Mike's lap.

'Whap, Whap, Whap, Whap, Whap'

"Ahhhhh, shit, shit, shit! Fuck!" Cory reeled then, as it seemed that Mike was whapping him harder than Joe had done. "That shit hurts, man!"

'Whap, Whap, Whap, Whap, Whap'

The two ushers chuckled meanly, and Mike said, "Well, it isn't supposed to be ticklish, Cory boy..."

...and *'Whap, Whap, Whap, Whap, Whap'*

"Owwwwww! God!" Cory yelled, pressing his palms hard against the carpeted floor and the toes section of his patent leather lace-up shoes against the floor behind him. "C'mon, you guys, it's my wedding day. Give me a break here!" Cory was tormented.

As Mike whapped and whapped the stuffing out of Cory's ass, turning it a bright shade of red, Joe said, "No way, Cory, your dad said to go hard on you. He wants you to always know that even though you're now married, he still plans to keep you on the straight and narrow."

"Owwwww! Lucky me!" Cory cried, tears forming in his eyes at that point and his cock churning all the more as it hung between Mike's legs.

After Mike had paddled him just as nearly as many times as Joe had, the groom again found himself back over Joe's lap.

At that point, his tears were flowing profusely, and his ass felt as if he had sat on a hot waffle iron. It stung.

As Joe rubbed his leather paddle over and over Cory's reddened ass cheeks, the groom hacked back a sniffle and said, in a panicked tone of voice, "Hey, what, what will I tell Kathleen when I get back to the dais? I told her I only needed to wash my hands before we ate. I've been gone pretty long for a guy who just came down here to wash his hands..."

As he rubbed the paddle some more over Cory's buttocks, Joe asked him, "And did you wash your hands when you got down here?"

"Yeah, I did, after I had pissed," Cory responded, and Mike tittered, "Uh-oh..."

"What do you mean uh-oh?" Cory asked through his tears.

"You told Kathleen you were coming here to wash your hands," Mike said. "Did you tell her you were also going to urinate?"

"N-no, I-I didn't..." Cory said.

"Oh no, oh no, Cory," Joe said as he went on rubbing the paddle over the groom's ass cheeks. "You lied to your new wife. You told her you were coming here to wash your hands, but you didn't tell her you were going to urinate as well. What would your Dad do in this situation, Cory?"

"B-but Dad taught me never to announce that I had to relieve myself when I would have to leave the table!" Cory pleaded.

"Kathleen is your wife. There's no reason you could have told her you needed to relieve yourself," Mike said. "Looks like your Dad needs to make some modifications."

Smiling, Joe looked up at Mike and said, "I'll begin making the modifications right now. Cory, again, I ask you, what would your Dad do in this situation?

Cory clenched his teeth, his cock churned like crazy, and he softly said, "My, my Dad would add another round of paddling to my punishment. *Shit!*"

Joe hooked a strong arm around Cory, pressed the young man against him, raised his paddle, and then he started all over again!

'*Whap, Whap, Whap, Whap, Whap*'

"Awwwwwwwh, oh God! Owwwwwwwwwwwww!" Cory screamed now.

"We were each going to give you two rounds of paddling, Cory," Joe said as he whapped and whapped the groom's ass. "But seeing as we caught you in a lie, we're going to have to do what your Dad would do. You'll get a third round from each of us."

'*Whap, Whap, Whap, Whap, Whap, Whap, Whap, Whap*'

"Ow, oh poor me, and you two are only up to your second round each of paddling me!" Cory cried miserably, his face tear-soaked at that point. "Oweeeeee! Please finish already. My newlywed wife must be waiting for me. It's my wedding day, for God's sake." Cory pleaded in pain.

'*Whap, Whap, Whap, Whap, Whap*'

"M-my ass will be minced meat by the time you guys are done giving me three rounds each! Ow!" Cory screamed loudly.

As Joe went on paddling Cory for his second round, Mike said, "You obviously don't know just how much punishment a man's ass can take."

'*Whap, Whap, Whap, Whap, Whap*'

"Owwwwwwwwww! Growing up with my dad, I do know, I do know just how much punishment a man's ass can take, "Owwwwwwwwww!" Cory wailed.

Later, when Cory reappeared back in the gala room where his and Kathleen's wedding was being celebrated he was making his way to the dais when his Dad came up to him.

"Where have you been, Cory?" the groom's father, a handsome gentleman with salt and pepper hair, asked his son. "It's nearly time for the mother and son dance."

Still sniveling a bit, his ass cheeks totally purpled, and his cock still churning, despite the severe paddling's he had suffered, the groom looked at his father and said, "Y-you know where I've been, Dad. You sent my two ushers to paddle my ass because you decreed that a man's wedding day is the perfect day to redden his ass. Well, your two lackeys did more than redden my ass; they turned it as purple as an eggplant. I won't be able to sit for a week or more, probably."

With a look of confusion on his face, Cory's Dad said, "I have no idea what you're talking about, son. I sent no one to paddle you. I mean, yes, I did give Joe and Mike leather paddles as party favors after your bachelor party, but I never told them to paddle you, not here at your wedding or any other time for that matter."

Cory's jaw dropped...

"Now then, before *I do* decide to tan your behind here at your wedding, let the DJ know you're back so he can announce the mother and son dance," Cory's dad said with total authority. "To think you would accuse me of such a thing on of all days. We will talk about this down the line, Cory."

"Y-yes, Dad. Yes, sir." Cory stammered, and as his father walked off, the groom looked over at where his two ushers, Joe and Mike, were sitting, and they were looking at him and laughing hysterically.

/The End/

A Soldier Tells His Story

OKAY, YOU GUYS, now that the card game is over and we've all enjoyed our beer; I feel it's time to share a story with you. It's something I never thought I would tell anyone about, but you guys are my best friends in the world, and I know I can trust you completely. Besides, I've kept it inside me for so long that I feel I have to finally say it. The story takes place during my time in the army when I was just a young, patriotic twenty-year-old. My sergeant had granted me a three-day pass, and I decided to visit my parents. I boarded a Greyhound bus and arrived home around 7:30 on a Friday evening. Naturally, my parents were bursting with pride. They were so proud of me. I mean, there I stood in my crisp uniform, looking clean-cut, handsome, and in great shape – an absolute contrast to how I had been in high school.

After a delicious and satisfying dinner, I retreated to my old room, bringing along two chilled beers with me. Having already consumed a couple of beers during dinner, I was feeling quite relaxed. It was a warm and pleasant night, so I opened my bedroom window wide, leaving only the shade pulled down. I stripped out of my uniform down to my fatigue-style briefs and black calf-length dress socks. I stretched out on my comfortable four-poster bed with my beers and the TV on.

When I was done with the two beers, I went to the bathroom, pissed like a fucking racehorse, went back to my bedroom, turned off the TV, and lay down on the bed. In moments, I succumbed to a deep sleep. The alcohol from the beers I had consumed resulted in a sound slumber, rendering me unaware of the faint sounds outside – the four individuals cautiously making their way into my room through the open bedroom window.

It was Lester, Victor, Dennis, and Howard – these were four guys I had known since childhood. They were sort of like friends, but mostly, they always delighted in bullying me. That particular night, they made their way into my room and around my bed, gawking hungrily at me as I slept soundly.

"Man, Mickey boy looks damned fucking good since he joined the service," I vaguely heard Dennis say, as though I were dreaming. "Look at that fucking body... muscles galore..."

Victor chimed in, also whispering, "Yeah, and that fucking bulge in his army briefs is telling a story."

It was an eerie sensation, strange – I could hear their words even while I was asleep. Like I said, I thought I was dreaming, a distorted reality. Howard, squatting down next to one of my socked feet, took in a deep, exaggerated, heavy sniff.

"His feet sure do stink," Howard whispered.

Breaking his silence, Lester spoke harshly, revealing their sinister intentions, "Look, we have to get this fucker tied up before we can do anything. Dennis, did you put rope in that backpack of yours?"

Dennis smiled fiendishly as he unzipped the backpack he was carrying over his shoulders. He pulled out a few lengths of rope and handed some to each of the guys.

"Okay, let's do this quick and quiet," Lester whispered.

Each of the four guys assisted in tying me to my bed. The rope was around each of my wrists and ankles and tied off to the four posts of the bed. I was in a spread-eagle position; every goddamned part of me was a target for the four jokers. As they tied me, Howard stole a lick at one of my socked feet. Helpless and vulnerable, my entire body was at the mercy of their malevolent intentions.

My body reacted instinctively, jerking in response to the sudden sensation. In haste, the guys cinched the knots, binding me securely to my bed.

"Man, we are going to have some serious fun!" Lester taunted.

I started to wake up, but by then, it was too late. I abruptly realized the dire situation I was in! I was securely tied to my bed and helpless. What woke me up in full was the fact that Dennis and Howard were each squatting at the ends of the bed, licking my damned stinking feet. I opened my eyes, and the first thing I saw was Lester's face looming over me.

"Shit!" I yelled. "What the absolute fuck is happening here?"

When I tried to get up off the bed, I became aware of the fact that I was tied to it.

"Lester, you despicable bastard!" I seethed at him. "Nothing fucking changes, does it?"

"Lower your voice, Soldier boy, or I'll be forced to gag you with my sweat socks," Lester said as he gently stroked my short brown hair. "We don't want your parents hearing any of what's going on in here. Imagine if they were to come in here and find their handsome soldier boy son all roped to his bed in his briefs and socks. It could be really embarrassing for you."

I looked down and saw Dennis and Howard, each hungrily licking, kissing, and sucking one of my feet.

"Shit!" I rasped. "Those two perverts are fucking licking my stinking feet! Untie me now, *you shitheads!*"

But of course, they ignored me, and as I struggled to pull free of the ropes, Victor began lapping at my big testicles, which were still in my army briefs.

"OOOOOOOO...oh my God..." I huffed.

Lester stopped stroking my hair and leaned down over my nipples. He took one of them into his mouth and began heartily sucking it.

"Shit, you four went from being bullies to being goddamned faggots!" I ranted angrily.

Then, the tip of my erect cock peeked out of the top of my briefs. I could not believe it was oozing pre-cum.

"Boy, oh boy, Soldier boy, for someone who hates all this so much, that cock of yours is surely saying something very different," Victor said, looking up at me, "It looks like it's ready to shoot a monster-sized load."

"*Fuckers...*" I whispered.

Dennis and Howard continued licking my socked feet, running their fingers over and into the tops of my socks and snapping the elastic in them against my skin. They bent my feet forward and sucked on my toes, cradling my feet in their hands. It wasn't long before my socks were soaked in saliva, but the two men continued licking them.

My testicles were now aching from the constant pressure of Victor's tongue working them, and my nipple that was in Lester's mouth was by then erect and all red. Fuck! I have to admit I wanted to shoot that fucking load that Victor had mentioned earlier. But the four bullies were going to make me wait. And they had other things in mind for me at that. Lester joined Victor at my testicles, and the two men really tongued my nuts hard, even meanly snapping their fingers against them.

"RRRRRRR..." I seethed in pain through clenched teeth.

I could have called out for help, but honestly, I did not want my parents to hear a thing. It was humiliating enough what was happening to me. I squirmed helplessly on the bed and watched the four men continue to work me over. Lester and Victor switched from my testicles to my nipples, sucking and biting one of them each.

"You fuckers!" I said miserably. "What's the point of all this? You Bastards! Let me go!"

"Hey, when we're done here, let's each keep one of his socks as a souvenir of this!" Dennis said to Howard.

"You can have my damned socks!" I ranted, "Just untie me and get yourselves out of here!"

But then, Lester placed his hand on my throbbing cock and began stroking it.

"Oh shit...oh no..." I moaned. "Y-you're going to make me shoot my damned load..."

And shoot it, I did...right into my army briefs.

"OOOOOOOOO...yeah, yeah!" I moaned in ecstasy and anger at the same time.

My cum drenched the front of my briefs, and Victor and Lester smiled evilly across my chest at each other.

A while later, I found myself standing on top of my bed with my hands now tied tightly behind me and a blindfold tied over my eyes. I balanced myself awkwardly on the bed as the four bullies began round two of my torment. Victor and Lester knelt at my crotch, pulled my army briefs down in the front, and went to work lapping my cum out of them, licking and tonguing my testicles, and giving my semi-hard cock a few sucks every few moments. I grunted in pain and ecstasy at the same time. At my feet, Dennis and Howard were holding me steady by my ankles and having a grand ol' time licking my now saliva-soaked socks. I clenched my teeth in anger.

"Fuckers, perverts..." I seethed, "I'll kill you all for this shit!"

"Kill us?" Lester laughed. "Mickey, my soldier boy, by the time we're done with you, you'll be begging us to come back every night while you're home on leave."

With that, he slurped my cock into his mouth again...

"UUUUHHHHH..." I grunted.

As Lester sucked my cock, Victor pulled one of my testicles into his mouth and worked on it hard. I did my damnedest not to yell out in pain for fear of my parents hearing me.

As Lester sucked me faster and faster, I knew I was close to shooting a second load of white gooey hot cum!

"Oh Good God..." I seethed through clenched teeth. "I'm going to fuckin' shoot another load!"

This time when I came, Lester swallowed it, *every damned drop...*

"Ohhhhhhhh!" I moaned loudly.

I shook in ecstasy on the bed as my four captors held me steady and balanced. Finally, I caught my breath, and the four bullies retied me to my bed, back in a spread-eagle position. The blindfold was removed, and I watched as Dennis and Howard (those two-foot hungry perverts) went back to work, licking, lapping, sucking, and biting on my still-socked feet. Victor and Lester each took one of my sore nipples into their mouths and again began working them hard.

"You bastards..." I said in exhaustion.

I lay there at their mercy, my cock and balls sticking out of my army briefs.

After another 15 minutes or so of licking my feet, working my nipples, and teasing my cock and balls, all four of the bullies whipped their cocks out of the fly holes in their jeans.

"Okay, Soldier boy Mickey, now it's your turn," Lester said. "Move away from his feet, guys, and Victor and I will give you something to lick off them."

Dennis and Howard stopped licking my feet and stepped away from them. Victor and Lester positioned their big cocks over my feet and began jacking themselves off. Watching them stroke those big pulsing cocks caused my cock to get hard again.

"Shit..." I rasped. "Fuckers are going to cream on my damned socks..."

And sure enough, that's exactly what the fuck they did. Lester and Victor each shot a giant load onto one of my feet each.

"Oh yeah, yeah..." the two men moaned, "Oh fucking yes..."

They forced every possible drop of cum from their piss slits, and their juices dripped over my socked toes and onto the front and back of my socked feet.

"Okay, you two, foot freaks, get busy..." Lester said to Dennis and Howard.

Dennis and Howard quickly resumed their positions at my feet and began licking the cum off my socks.

"Looks like we're going to be here a while more, Soldier boy Mickey..." Lester said as he grabbed my hard cock.

"Acch! Shit!" I rasped as Lester's hand encircled my manhood.

Lester gobbled my cock back into his mouth again as Victor resumed torturing one of my nipples with his mouth.

It took a good while this time, but, unbelievably, I did shoot a third load. Fucking cum hungry Lester swallowed it again. I writhed in ecstasy, and by then, Dennis and Howard were done licking Victor and Lester's cum off my socks. But they still weren't done using and abusing me. Dennis and Howard each whipped their cocks out of their jeans and began stroking themselves over my damned feet.

"Oh no, *not again,*" I said.

As Dennis and Howard stroked their big slabs of meat, Lester and Victor watched intently. At least they had stopped sucking my cock and my nipples. I mean, don't get me wrong. Having your cock sucked, and your nipples worked feels great, but after shooting three damned loads in a short span of time, I was feeling pretty sore. Fuck that, that last load was forced from me. Dennis and Howard each shot a wad of cum from their piss holes and onto my socks.

"OH YEAH FUCKS YEAH..." they both panted as they, like Lester and Victor, forced every drop of cum from themselves.

When they were done, they squatted back at my feet and began licking their cum off them.

"Man, those two really are foot fiends," Lester quipped to Victor.

"You're all fiends!" I squawked miserably.

The four men laughed. Finally, Dennis and Howard were done licking their cum off my socked feet. They untied my feet, and Dennis and Howard each rolled one of my black and smelly socks off my feet. They stuffed my socks into their jeans pockets as Victor slid my army briefs off me and put them in his jeans pocket.

"What's the matter, Lester?" I asked him sarcastically. "You're not taking anything to remember me by?"

"I got your cum, twice," Lester sneered at me, "That's the best trophy I can take!"

With that, the four bullies tucked their big cocks back into their jeans, untied my wrists, and I watched in exhaustion as they left my bedroom through the window. I fell asleep and slept through the rest of the night.

My story finished. I leaned back in my chair and looked at my three-card-playing and beer-drinking buddies.

"Man, those four dudes really worked you over big time, Mickey," my friend Ralph said to me, sounding astonished.

"Yeah, they sure as hell did," I agreed.

"Did you ever have a chance to get even with them?" my friend Robert asked me.

"Nah," I said, "To tell you the truth, I never saw them again."

"I have one question..." my friend Irving said, looking at me intently across the table.

"Shoot..." I said.

"How can we earn your socks as a souvenir of this card game?" he asked me.

"Shit..." I said with a sly smile on my face.

/The End/

Paul's Nipples

MY NAME IS PAUL, I work as a construction worker for a company called "Greene and Sons Construction Corp." What I want to tell you about happened last summer in the scorching heat of August. I stand about six feet tall, with short brown hair, big green eyes, and I'm built like a brick shit house from working all day every day at my construction job.

As I said, it was August, and two of my buddies and I were working on the concourse level of an office building. We were renovating an office down there. I was dressed in worn blue jeans, a tight-fitted white tank top, and calf-length scuffed-up construction boots. With all the power off and no ventilation in the concourse, we did not even have air conditioning, and we were sweating like pigs in that heat. The only source of light we had was from our high-powered battery-operated lamps, which were set up all over the room. My tank top was drenched with sweat, causing my big nipples to be popping out, pressing against the white cotton material.

My work buddies always teased the stuffing out of me about my big nipples, telling me that my tits looked better and bigger than a woman's. Sometimes, in good fun, they would even playfully pinch or squeeze my nipples through my shirt. On particularly hot days, when I worked shirtless, my friends would take it a step further and twist my nipples. Although it may sound unusual, I didn't mind their antics, as it was all done in the spirit of harmless fun among friends. In fact, even some of the girls I've dated have found my nipples to be quite erotic, heh! One girl spent the better part of an evening sucking my nipples like crazy. It felt great, to say the least. I've often wondered how many guys are missing out on the great feeling of having their nipples worked on. Anyhow, it was the end of the workday, and my two buddies and I were ready to call it a day. They were busy working on a wall as I was installing hinges on a door. They stopped their work and looked over at me.

"Quittin' time, Pauly boy," Mike called over to me.

"Yeah, it sure as shit is," I replied, "I'm going to stay and finish this door, and then I'll be on my way."

They stepped over to where I was working and looked at the door.

"If you want, we can stay and help you finish it," Mike said to me.

"Nah, I'll do it," I replied, concentrating on the work, wanting to finish it off as soon as possible and head home.

"Looking to rack up on that overtime, eh Pauly boy?" Billy asked me, and as expected, he gave one of my nipples a fast squeeze.

"Sure as shit!" I said with a smile.

"Okay, Paul. See you tomorrow," Mike said, and when he and Billy left, I resumed working on the door.

Around five minutes later, I heard footsteps out in the corridor.

"Hey!" I yelled, thinking it was Mike and Billy, "Are you two still here?"

The footsteps stopped, but I heard no response to my question. I stopped what I was doing and called out again, "Mike! Billy? Is that you two?"

Still no reply, I walked slowly out to the corridor.

"Hey, you guys, I know you're still here 'cause I heard you stomping around," I said, standing in the center of the corridor, feeling agitated.

Suddenly, from behind me, two guys snuck up on me and quickly grabbed my arms in what felt like vise-like grips.

"Uuulllpppp!" I sputtered.

"Got him, Cleeve!" the guy on my left said with a sadistically gleeful tone in his voice, "And just look at him. We struck gold this time!"

"WH-who are you two?" I asked them, struggling in their beyond-strong grasp. "What in all fucks is this? Let me go!"

"C'mon, let's get this stack of beef and muscles back in that room and find something to tie him to!" Cleeve said.

Using two huge hands each on my arms, they lifted me effortlessly off the floor and lugged me back to my work area.

"Bastards! Tie me to something?" I roared, "Put me the fuck down!"

I swung my legs out in front of me, trying to free myself from their mighty grasp, but man, *were they strong!*

"Fuck, he's a stubborn and mighty one, Otis," Cleeve said to his friend.

"I see some heavy-duty rope over there on the floor," Otis said, "Right under that wooden post."

They carried me, kicking and struggling over to the post, and put me down against it, meanly yanking my arms behind me and around the post.

"Uuuuuhhhhh!" I snarled. "Fuckers!"

They pulled my arms back as far as possible, meanly twisting them at the same goddamned time.

"Aaarrrrhhhhh!" I snarled in pain, anger, and terror as well, "*What in all fucks do you guys want?*"

"Hold his wrists tight, Otis," Cleeve said, "I'm going to grab some rope."

Cleeve let go of my arm that he was holding, and Otis grabbed both my wrists in his hands. He held them tightly behind me, just as one holds onto his jackpot, as Cleeve picked up a long length of rope.

"No, no!" I yelled, struggling to free myself from Otis' grip, knowing they were going to tie me the fuck up.

My mind was reeling with questions. "*Is this a joke? Am I going to be robbed?*"

"What in all fucking fucks is going on here?" I was startled.

Then, I felt the rope being wound round and round my wrists and to the post I was standing against. In moments, my wrists were securely bound behind me and to the post. The two burly men squatted down in front of me and tied the rope around my feet over my construction boots. When they were done, the one named Otis ran a hand over my tied feet.

"Nice pick, eh Cleeve?" he asked his friend.

"Sure is Otis," Cleeve agreed, "I'm glad you spotted him working here. And I'm even gladder he decided to work late."

At that moment, I knew what they were after. *Fuck.* I swallowed hard.

"Y-you two are faggots!" I roared as they stood up in front of me.

"Watch your mouth, hot guy!" Cleeve said to me. "I wouldn't want to mess up that pretty face of yours."

"Look at those nips of his, Cleeve," Otis said, running the palm of his hand over my well-toned chest. "Real big titties he's got. *All day suckers!*"

"Or all night..." Cleeve said lustfully, giving one of my nipples a hard squeeze through my shirt, just like my work buds would do, but these two slobs were not my work buds. *Fuck!*

"Fucking perverts..." I seethed at them.

Otis pulled my tank top out of my jeans and slowly rolled it up my torso till my big nipples were on display.

"Fuck, those tits look good enough to fucking eat!" Cleeve exclaimed.

The two men each took one of my nipples in their thumb and first fingers. They squeezed and twisted the tips of them, torturing me erotically, it can be said. Straight as I am, I felt my big cock reacting in my jeans. If these two jokers thought that my nipples were going to be a treat, just wait until they saw my cock, I thought to myself. I mean, I'm eight inches down there when I'm not erect. As they teased my nipples with their fingers, I struggled like a madman to pull free of the ropes. Unfortunately, it was useless. I was tied up too fucking tight.

"Fucking bastards!" I yelled at them.

Then, when my nipples were erect, hard, and pointy, the two men leaned down, and they each slurped one of my nubs into their mouths. They began sucking them, swirling their tongues on them, and lightly chewed on the tender flesh.

"Ooohh...Fuck!" I moaned and arched my head back; looking up at the ceiling and the back of my head now against the post I was bound to, enjoying yet wondering what in the fuck was happening.

I was loathe to admit it, but it felt so fucking good as they slurped madly on my nipples like two nursing babies. They ran their hands over my muscular arms, squeezed my well-built biceps, and sucked my nipples some more at the same time.

The slurping sounds - like a kid with a lollipop, they were making were actually driving me crazy! Their saliva dripped down my chest as they drooled over my nipples. Then, with their front-most teeth, they bit down lightly on my nubs and pulled on them.

"Aaarrrhhh!" I cried and looked down at what the fuck they were doing. "Fuck, easy with my nipples, you crazy guys!"

In response, they each gave my pecs a hard slap each.

"Owww!" I grunted loudly.

My cock was now hard as steel in my jeans. The tent it was making would be noticed by the two men soon enough, and then they would no doubt chow down on that next. *Oh God No!*

But for the moment, they were pretty contented with my big man-sized nipples. They stopped biting on them and wrapped only their lips around them now. They teased them with the tips of their tongues as their lips kissed them.

"Ooohh...fucking faggots..." I whispered breathlessly. "Eatin' my damned tits..."

I thought how if I had left earlier with Mike and Billy, I wouldn't be in this damned mess now. *Oh, how I wish I wouldn't have stayed!*

Roped to a post and having my nipples eaten and feasted on by two giant faggots. Otis ran his hand up behind my neck and caressed it as he sucked the nipple he had in his mouth. Cleeve was still running his hand over my arm as he sucked on the nipple he had in his mouth. And it wasn't long before my nipples were feeling sore, numb, and pained, all at the same time.

"Guys, please, how about giving it a break, huh?" I pleaded with them.

They ignored me and sucked my nipples harder and harder.

"Aaaaarrrrhhhh!" I loudly roared as they bit harshly down on my sore nipples.

Then, Cleeve's hand found my hard-on. He stopped sucking my nipple and looked down at the huge tent in my jeans.

"Fuck Otis, *look at this...*" Cleeve said breathlessly.

Otis ceased sucking my other nipple and looked down where Cleeve was pointing. I looked down at my nipples and saw that they were more than erect. They were red, swollen, and aching. But now I had another problem.

"Goddamn, that piece of meat in his jeans must be eleven fucking inches long!" Otis said breathlessly yet excitedly.

"Let's find out..." Cleeve said anxiously.

Together, they unbuttoned my jeans and yanked them down to my knees, revealing my white Calvin Klein briefs. They ran their hands over my briefs, snapped the elastic in them, and squeezed the hard-on I was sporting in them.

"Damned fuckers...*leave my cock alone...*" I said angrily.

Cleeve reached into the back of my briefs and gave my bubble butt a hard squeeze.

"Aaaarhhh..." I grunted.

"Fuck, this guy is real fucking hot!" Cleeve said to Otis, a look of triumph on his face.

Otis brazenly pulled my hard, *hard* cock out of the fly opening of my briefs, along with my big juicy testicles. The two men stared in awe at my meat stick. Like a fucking hotdog it was!

I was long, hard, fat, and throbbing. Pre-cum was oozing from my sexy slit, and my testicles were hanging down real low, chock filled with my manly spunk. Otis hunkered down and ran his tongue over the side of my cock, and licked my testicles.

"Oooh, yeah..." I moaned in passion.

"Fucking hot guy is enjoyin' this, Cleeve," Otis said.

"Goddamn, I can't wait any longer, Otis..." Cleeve said breathlessly, "I have to shoot a fucking load now!"

"Yeah, me too, Cleeve..." Otis agreed and stood up straight.

They both extracted their cocks from their jeans and began stroking them. My God, their cocks were big and fat too.

"Fuckers, cocks are almost as big as mine..." I murmured.

They stroked themselves faster and faster, grunted in heated passion, and squeezed my nipples at the same time. Then, they shot their loads, shooting giant pent-up loads of hot creamy sperm.

"Oooh yeah fucking A man!" Cleeve screamed in a man's passion.

"Yeah, Yeah, fucking A man is right!" Otis chimed in.

They shot their tremendous loads all over the front of my briefs and on my cock, drenching my manhood with their juices. It felt so warm as it landed on my cock. Some of it landed on my construction boots, and I had visions of the two men licking it off them. When they were done, they slid their spent cocks back into their jeans, catching their breath as they did so.

"Oh man, that was fucking good," Otis panted.

"Oh yeah, you got that right," Cleeve agreed, "and we still have our hot guy."

They both squatted down at my cock and licked all the cum off it, a little at a time, sending shivers through my well-muscled body. They took turns sucking my cock, feeding it to each other. They squeezed my testicles a few times, and I knew *I* would soon shoot a load.

"Ooohhh yeah, suck my big cock, you bastards. Eat that meat of mine!" I found myself whispering breathlessly and enjoying.

They teased my sexy slit with the tips of their tongues and ran their hands over my cum soaked briefs at the same time.

"Ooohhhhh fuck, yeah..." I grunted crazily.

They sucked me as if their lives depended on it after a while, and then I felt myself at what I refer to as the boiling point.

"Oh yeah, you fucking guys, I'm cumming. *I'm fucking cumming now!*" I roared with passion.

They stopped sucking my cock and bolted to their feet. I stood rigidly and tensely against the post I was roped to and fucking shot my load as the two men squeezed my sore nipples hard.

"Awwww yeah...oh yeah!" I roared, watching in amazement as my sperm shot from my cock, without my cock even being touched at that point. "Shootin' my fucking load... yeah!"

It seemed like I would not stop cumming, as more and more hot white juice spewed from my sexy slit. And all the while, Cleeve and Otis went on squeezing my nipples. When I was done, I leaned my head down to catch my breath.

"Feelin' good there, hot guy?" Cleeve asked me.

"Hell yeah..." I replied, "How about untying me now, guys?"

Instead, they packed my cock and testicles back into my briefs and again slurped my nipples into their mouths.

"Ooooooo God...*you fuckers...*" I moaned helplessly.

After I've shot a big load, it seems as if my entire body becomes super sensitive to the touch, especially my damned nipples. At that moment, I didn't want the two degenerates touching my nipples, let alone to be sucking them again. But I was powerless to stop them, so I was forced to endure the torture.

"Bastards..." I grunted.

Like earlier, they worked my nipples with their tongues, swirling them all over my nubs. They bit down on them with their front teeth and pulled on them, yanking them forward. I was afraid they were going to literally rip my poor tortured nipples right off my chest. They ran their hands over my rock-hard chest, squeezing it as they slurped and sucked on my nipples like crazy. Now, if you're at all like me, after shooting a big load of cream, the need to piss becomes overpowering. My cock began to grow what I call piss hard.

"Hey, you two tit-hungry bastards, you'd better untie me now," I grumbled, looking down at them. "I really have to piss."

They ignored me and continued working on my nipples, torturing them.

"*Bastards!*" I said again, whispering this time.

I held it for as long as I could but then realized I couldn't hold it anymore.

As Cleeve and Otis sucked my nipples, I pissed.

"Ooohhhh fuck, fuck..." I grunted in humiliation. Fucking pissing in my damned briefs.

The fronts and sides of my briefs were suddenly sopped in piss as I relieved myself. It mixed with the cum that was on them, and I was able to smell the hot funky mixture. Aarghhh! Then, Cleeve stopped sucking on my nipple that he had in his mouth, took it between his thumb and first finger, and looked at Otis.

"You know Otis, when we're done here, those briefs of his will make a real kinky souvenir," Cleeve said.

"I agree," Otis said after taking his mouth off my other nipple.

My nipples were beyond sore at that point. They seemed to have turned red, and they looked as if they were ready to explode right off my big chest. God, it hurt! Cleeve leaned in close to me and pressed his mouth against mine. Unbelievably, I found myself responding to the man's kiss as his huge tongue invaded my mouth. I puckered my lips and swirled my tongue into his mouth. He pressed his hands against my face as he kissed me hard on the mouth.

"Fucking hot guy is kissing you, Cleeve," Otis quipped, "He really is getting off on all this."

Cleeve stopped kissing me and looked at Otis.

"Yeah, Otis, he sure is," Cleeve agreed heartily, "We sure as all fuck did pick a winner this time."

Smiling fiendishly, they both resumed sucking my nipples.

"Oooh no, no...please guys...enough with my damned tits already," I begged.

As they worked my nipples some more, I tried desperately to pull myself free of the ropes binding my wrists. As I struggled through, my cock grew hard again in my briefs. I could not fucking believe it. After this was over, I would have a lot to think about. I mean, was I really aroused over all this? I mean, there I was, tied to a post with my pants down around my knees while two faggots slurped and sucked my nipples. I had kissed one of them. I mean, really fucking kissed him. Yeah, and now my cock was erect again. I really would have a lot to think about when this was over. Cleeve's hand roamed over my body as he worked the nipple he had in his mouth, and then he found my hard-on. He squeezed it through my soaked briefs and stroked it a few times.

"Fucker..." I said breathlessly. "Going to make me shoot my load again."

As the two men sucked my nipples more and more, Cleeve slowly stroked my cock through the cotton material of my briefs. I was sweating like mad now and shaking in forced ecstasy. Sweat rolled off my chest and down to my nipples. The two tit-hungry bastards slurped up my sweat and went right on sucking my nipples. I was in pain now and ecstasy at the same fucking time. And I was getting close to shooting a second load, this time right into my briefs.

"Oooooo, you fucker..." I said breathlessly. "Getting real close now."

Cleeve stroked me faster and faster, and then, "Oooooo yeah, fucking again!" I rasped in a high-pitched tone of voice. *"Fucking creaming in my briefs!"*

I slammed my head against the post as the two men sucked my nipples as hard as possible, causing me to shoot more into my briefs. Cleeve squeezed every possible drop from my cock and then let go of my manhood. They stopped sucking my nipples, and once again, I stood, catching my breath.

"Bastards..." I whispered, *"Fucking bastards..."*

They slapped my flat stomach region and laughed, telling me how I was enjoying every moment of it all. Then, they extracted their hard cocks from their jeans and stroked them, pointing them at me.

"Ooooohhhh yeah hot guy..." Cleeve groaned, "Watching you shoot that second load makes me want to shoot a second one."

"Me too..." Otis said to me.

They shot their loads a few moments later, shooting their cum all over my briefs. At that point, my damned briefs were soaked with piss, cum, and sweat. When the two men were done, they packed their big cocks back into their jeans and ran their mangy hands over my chest, squeezing my sore, red nipples at the same time.

"Please, please no more..." I pleaded. *"I-I can't take it."*

"A big, strong guy like you can't take it?" Cleeve asked me, "C'mon, hot guy, we have plenty of time, and you're in no position at all to be telling us what the fuck to do."

They leaned down and slurped my poor nipples back into their mouths *again*.

"Oh no, no, no, no, no, no, no, no, no, no, no, no, no, no, no, no, no," I whimpered helplessly.

Tears of pain formed in my eyes and flowed freely down my cheeks. They worked me over until the middle of the night, finally leaving around 3:00 am. They ripped my briefs off me, and indeed, they took them as a kinky souvenir. They left me tied to the post, laughing and cackling as they left the building. I tried desperately to pull free of the ropes, but it was impossible. My nipples and cock were beyond sore. I had shot another load of cum, and Cleeve and Otis had sucked my nipples past soreness. If I didn't get myself free of the ropes, my buddies would find me this way. But unfortunately, I did not manage to get myself untied, and 7:00 am rolled around. I was still tied to the post with my tank top rolled up past my nipples, my jeans down around my knees, and my cock and testicles on display when Mike and Billy came in the room. At the sight of me, their eyes opened wide as saucers.

"Holy shit!" Mike exclaimed, "Pauly boy, what in all fucks are you doing roped to that post?"

"It's a long and fucked up story, guys," I replied, "and it was a long night. Please, untie me. My arms are all numb."

They walked over to me and looked me over.

"Shit Pauly boy, where are your underpants?" Billy asked me, giving my cock a quick feel.

"And look at those nipples," Mike said, staring in wonder at my sore nubs, "What the fuck happened?"

"T-two guys, fucking faggots, busted in here last night after you two went home," I told them. "They grabbed me, overpowered me, tied me the fuck up to this post, and fucking worked me over as if I were a sex toy. They fucking sucked my tits until I thought they were going to bite them off my chest, and they forced me to shoot my load a few times. They took my damned briefs as a souvenir. I would be willing to bet that they're sniffing them right now. *Shit...*"

Mike and Billy looked at each other and then back at me.

"They sucked your tits?" Mike asked me, *"All night long?"*

"Yeah, I've been here all night," I replied. "Please, untie me."

"You know Billy; we'll be the only ones here till about 9:00 am," Mike said to Billy, a fiendish look on his face, "Are you thinking what I'm thinking?"

"I sure am, buddy," Mike replied, "As we've always said, those nipples of his look better than a woman's."

They leaned down, and they each took one of my nipples into their mouths.

"Some fucking buds you two turned out to be!" I shouted as they sucked my nipples.

An hour later, Billy and Mike finally untied me. I took the day off to go home and get some rest. I haven't seen or heard from Cleeve or Otis since that day. I wonder sometimes if they're looking for me. Even though I'm straight every time a woman works my nipples, it's never quite the same as when those two big burly fuckers worked them. When I feel in the mood, I let Mike and Billy have at my nipples. Sometimes, they tie me up just to add to the fun. But overall, my nipples have caused me both pleasure and pain, and I've always loved every moment of it.

It was one unforgettable night!

/The End/

Dominick

I Work As A Construction Worker for a construction company. A couple of years back, when we were short-staffed, we hired some temps to work on a really big job for the company. One of the temps was a real macho dude named Randy. Fuck! I mean, Randy was so macho that he made me look like a goddamned pansy, and I'm about as macho as they come. Bald as a fucking eagle, I have intense-looking dark eyes. I'm built like a goddamned brick shit house from all the slinging of hammers and carrying of two-by-fours that I do nearly every day on the job and not to mention, but I work out at the gym with weights four days a week, but fuck it, I'll mention it. Not all too shabby for a guy in his mid-thirties, eh buds?

Anyway, Randy and I were partnered in the basement of the building we were working in, just the two of us - macho bald me and tall and muscular brown-haired, brown-eyed, twenty-something-year-old Randy. Just like any other two construction dudes working together, we started talking and chatting at first about general stuff like the weather, movies we liked, or whether we were married or not.

I told Randy that I had a beautiful Japanese wife named Kim and a one-year-old boy. Without looking at me as he was yanking a nail out of a wall with the claw-back of a hammer, Randy said, "I'm single, I'm gay, and I love to suck cock, especially construction worker's cock. And that's why I became a construction worker because, in every job I'm assigned to, I get to suck construction worker cock."

As Randy went on yanking and struggling to get the nail out of the wall, my jaw dropped, and a look of disbelief came over my mug.

"What, what in all fuck did you just say, bud?" I asked Randy incredulously.

He finally got the nail out of the wall, put his hammer down on a worktable, turned and looked at me head-on, and said, "I'm single, I'm gay, and I love to suck construction worker cock. That's why I became a construction worker."

Saying that, Randy took a couple of non-hesitant steps toward me.

"Is there any part of it that you didn't understand, Dominick?" Randy asked me, grinning from ear to ear.

"Jeez, man, I never..." I began, "I mean, I've heard of all the gay fantasies of gay men looking to suck off straight construction workers, straight cops, straight soldiers, but I never..."

"Never thought you'd hear a gay guy like me say it for real and, so outright?" Randy chuckled and took a few more steps toward me until we were standing face to face, boot toes to boot toes.

"I know what straight construction workers love. They love to have their cocks sucked," Randy said, and my eyes opened wide as saucers as he brazenly and without any hesitation whatsoever cupped my jeans-covered crotch in one of his big paw-like hands. "And you're no exception, Dominick, judging from how hard, *how very hard* you are right now," he added.

"I-I'm always hard Bud..." I stammered as the guy ran the pad of his thumb up and down the length of my erection in my jeans. "Like any other dude in his thirties, I'm always all horned up and..."

"You're always all horned up because most wives don't suck cock." Randy said, and to my further disbelief, he was using two hands, one to pull back the material over my jeans' zipper and the other hand to lower my zipper. And to my even further fucking shock, I was doing nothing. *Nothing to stop him.*

"Uh Randy, yeah, you're right on the money on that, and about the part that the wife doesn't like to suck cock. She uh..." I babbled and stammered stupidly in front of him.

"No need to explain, Dominick," Randy went on as he lowered my zipper all the way, "As I said, it's the reason I became a construction worker."

As I stood there breathing heavily, I watched and still did nothing to stop the guy as he used his fingers to extract my big erect baby maker from my white boxer briefs' fly opening along with my big kiwi-sized balls.

"Randy, I-I can't. I'm a straight so and so..." I said in a husky-sounding tone of voice as the guy was caressing my erection. "I got a wife...and...well..." I struggled to find the right words.

Randy chuckled as he held my mammoth-sized manhood in one hand and cupped my balls in the other. He said, "Yeah, all you straight so and so's say the same thing."

As the fucker spoke, his lips were grazing mine, and fuck of fucks, I didn't pull away.

"So uh, you...you want to uh, you want to suck my cock, bud?" I asked the guy, his lips pecking mine as I spoke.

"No, Dominick. I just took your cock and balls out of your jeans so I could admire their beauty," Randy replied, sounding silly, rubbing the pad of his thumb over my pre-cum oozing cock slit.

I chuckled a bit and tried once more to put off the inevitable by saying, "But...but Randy...my wife..."

With that, Randy let go of my cock and balls, took off the long red, sweaty bandanna he was wearing around his forehead, leaned in closer, and tied the bandanna over my eyes, fucking blindfolding me, knotting it in the back of my bald head.

"Hey, what are you doing, bud?" I asked as the dude plunged me into darkness.

"This way, you don't have to watch me suck your cock and your balls Dominick," Randy said. Soon, I felt his hands caressing my thighs. No doubt he had hunkered down in front of me.

"Huh?" I asked in astonishment but made no move to take the blindfold off.

"Just pretend it's your wife sucking you, Dominick," Randy repeated, and then I felt his nose pressed against my cock slit. Damn! He was sniffing it, "Mmm...nice sweaty cheesy construction worker scent."

"Nice way to describe how my manhood smells," I laughed.

Then, the fucking guy gobbled my skyscraper of an erection into his craw.

"Huhhhhhh..." was the sound I made as Randy's velvety feeling (that's the best way I can describe them) lips closed around my stalk, and he began sucking it.

I fell back against the wall and propped myself there as waves of ecstasy engulfed me, as Randy's mouth engulfed all of my manhood.

"Awww fuck, getting my cock sucked on company time, getting paid to have my cock sucked, what a hoot," I grunted breathlessly.

As the fucking guy sucked my cock some more, drooling over it as he did so, I next felt him tugging my big balls up and down.

"Yuhhhh...yeah, love to have my balls toyed with while being sucked," I grumbled throatily, "my wife never does this to me."

Randy took my cock out of his mouth for a moment, continued tugging my balls, and said, "Pretend I'm your wife, Dominick," and quickly slurped me back into his mouth and most greedily at that, I might add.

"Yuhhhh...fuck, yeah, my wife...*my wife*..." I said in a throaty tone of voice.

I placed my hands up behind my head, toyed with the knot in the blindfold that Randy had tied over my eyes, and sooner than I thought, began thrusting my hips, fucking the guy's mouth now.

"Aw yeah, suck my cock, my wife is sucking my cock, at last, my wife is sucking my cock," I ballyhooed breathlessly, picturing my Kim's mouth full of my tube steak and what a vision that was; let me tell ya!

I thrust harder and harder into Randy's mouth, but then he slid my cock out of his craw and began tongue-bathing my sweaty balls.

"Aw... aww fuck, like that old song used to say, *what a feeling!*" I gurgled crazily, "What a real fucking feeling!"

"Didn't want you to cum too quickly, Dominick," Randy said in a sing-song-sounding voice and then alternately sucked my balls.

"Uhhhhhhhh..." I gasped, pressed myself up harder against the wall, arched my head back, and went on playing with the knot in my blindfold. "Yeah, savor me, baby, fucking savor me!"

"Mmmm..." Randy crooned, vibrating his mouth around my testicle that he presently had in his mouth.

As the fucking guy worked his mouth magic on my balls, my cock grew harder. I could feel it pointing straight out and oozing massive droplets of my construction worker pre cum.

"Uhhhhhh...fuck...won't be able to hold back much longer," I muttered, almost breathlessly.

"In that case..." Randy said and once more gobbled my erection into his mouth, and that was all it took for me to shoot my load like gangbusters, like a cat in heat on a hot Saturday night, swearing at Randy like a goddamned captured marine as the fucking guy chowed down on my mess.

"Arrrrrhhhhh yeah, fucking fucks," I roared. "Haven't had a blast that felt like this in fucking ages...my wife...my fucking wife...*fucckk...*"

Randy slid his hands up and down my thighs as I seemed to go on spurting and cumming and spurting and cumming.

"Arrrrrhhhhh, feels like it'll never stop," I seethed, pressed myself up harder against the wall, and thrust and shoved my spurting cock in the guy's craw.

But as the saying goes, eventually, all good things come to an end. Finally, my cock was spent, my balls were drained. *Fuck!*

As my cock slid out of Randy's mouth, I pulled the blindfold down from my eyes and left it dangling around my big neck. I looked down at Randy, and he grinned up at me, remnants of my slop all over his lips. I saw that he had his cock in his hand and that he had shot his load as well, all over the floor in front of where he was kneeling in front of me. *Fuck,* the guy had obviously cum while sucking me off. He really did love sucking construction worker cock!

"Fuck, that was amazing, bud," I panted at him.

Randy got to his feet and said, "You're welcome, Dominick," undid the knot in the bandanna as it dangled around my neck, gave me a quick peck on the cheek, and then said, "I think we'd better get back to work."

As we packed our spent cocks back into our jeans, I said to Randy, "I'll be good for another load in an hour or so." We both laughed and then got back to work.

/The End/

Nash

MY NAME IS NASH. I work as a chef in a top-of-the-line restaurant in New York City. I'm also a superb baker. I went to school for both, being a top-rate chef and baker. I suppose it can be said that since I was a kid, cooking and baking were my passions. My mother wasn't the best cook in the world, and my dad worked long hours, so as I was growing up, I found myself doing a lot of my own cooking. As time went on, I realized how much I looked forward to it. Even at a young age, I was creating excellent dishes, and for baking, I followed recipes in books. My mother wasn't the least bit jealous that I was a better cook and baker than her; in fact, she enjoyed it because it saved her from having to cook...and bake.

Every once in a while, she brings her friends to the restaurant where I work to enjoy the dishes I create, along with the special desserts.

AND not just my special dishes are on the menu in the restaurant where I work, but the desserts I bake are there as well, everything from cream pies to fancy cakes to exotic pastries to a host of ethnic desserts...

I live in a huge loft in the downtown area of Brooklyn that I had converted into an apartment...with a huge kitchen where I prepare ALL of my desserts for the restaurant. Cooking the meals at the restaurant is time-consuming enough, so I do all the baking at home...and I have a huge refrigerator that the restaurant paid for, so I'm able to store the desserts and then have restaurant personnel come to my apartment to pick them up and transport them to the restaurant in a special refrigerated truck made just for that purpose.

I've been dating a beautiful young lady named Lorraine, who was actually a customer in the restaurant where I work. She was out for dinner with two of her girlfriends, and after dinner, she had asked to meet the chef and the baker of the desserts that she and her girlfriends had enjoyed so immensely. When she found out that the chef and the baker were the same person, she was even more intrigued and wanted even more to meet me.

Their waiter that night was my buddy Charles, and upon Lorraine's request, he made his way to the kitchen to get me so she could meet me. It wasn't the first time something like this had happened, and I was only too glad to meet someone who thought so highly of my creativity when it came to food and baked treats.

But when I made my way over to Lorraine's table, where she was seated with her two girlfriends, I instantly realized that this time, meeting a patron of the restaurant who appreciated my chef's delights was totally different...because Lorraine was easily one of the most beautiful women I had ever met. She had long, black flowing hair, beautiful dark eyes, and the softest, kindest features I had ever seen. I guessed her age to be in the late twenties or maybe close to my age, in her early thirties, and when Charles introduced her to me, and I shook hands with her, it wasn't lost on me on how tightly she held my hand in hers. She introduced her girlfriends as Anna and Maureen, but truthfully, I could not have cared less what her friends' names were because, as that old song said years ago, I only had eyes for Lorraine. I boldly asked her if I could possibly buy her dinner sometime, and she instantly said yes, both of us looking at each other as if it were love at first sight.

I took Lorraine to dinner the following Friday night after she had gotten off work at the bank where she worked as a manager of the credit department. I, of course, didn't take her to dinner in the restaurant I worked for, but we had a wonderful first date nonetheless...and we've been seeing each other ever since. So yeah, I'm one contented so and so, a successful chef and baker, and now dating a beautiful young lady...very content, I must say...

Recently, I invited a co-worker of mine over to my apartment to help me with some of the desserts for the restaurant, seeing as it was nearing the holiday season of Thanksgiving to Christmas and the demand for pumpkin pies, coconut custard pies, apple pies, and all sorts of other desserts were going to be needed in huge abundance...so I innocently figured a little help was needed.

I gave Greg, the assistant restaurant manager, the key to my apartment and told him that I would meet him there that Monday afternoon, right after I had finished my meeting with the restaurant owner and manager to discuss how many of each dessert they wanted me to prepare for the Thanksgiving Day crowd that they got every year at the restaurant. I had also given Greg the keys to my car along with a lengthy list of ingredients that I needed him to go to specialty gourmet stores to purchase for me. I was beyond elated that he was glad to help me. He was a real good buddy, a fantastic assistant manager, and co-worker...RIGHT...YEAH RIGHT...OH YEAH RIGHT!

So, on Monday afternoon around 3:00PM, dressed in a navy-blue suit, white shirt, burgundy tie, and black slip-on highly shined wingtips, I took the train back to my apartment from the restaurant. Greg had texted me at 1:00PM to let me know that he had returned to my place with all the ingredients that I would need for baking all the desserts I would be busy with for the next few days leading up to Thanksgiving... I texted back a huge thank you and said I would be at the apartment shortly, change out of my suit into some relaxing sweats and a tee shirt, and get busy baking.

When I arrived at my apartment, I let myself in and found all the tables I keep in the kitchen to inventory my baking supplies covered with all the ingredients I had asked Greg to purchase for me from various gourmet stores that cater to bakers such as myself.

Greg wasn't in the kitchen, so I figured he'd stepped away to use the bathroom, so I loosened my tie and looked over the jars and jars of ingredients he had purchased, murmuring, "Good, good, excellent, he got everything I needed and more..."

By more, I meant that Greg had purchased a few bottles of Bosco chocolate syrup, Mrs. Butterworth's syrup, and dozens more eggs than I had asked for...and canned soups...

Canned soups? What did I need canned soups for, for making desserts...?

"Greg?" I called out toward the bathroom, "You here, bud?"

He didn't reply. I pulled my tie down a few notches and unbuttoned the top two buttons of my shirt. I saw on another table bottles of ketchup, soy sauce, jarred tomato sauce (JARRED TOMATO SAUCE? NEVER BUDS, NEVER...), and a variety of other jarred things I hadn't asked Greg to purchase... There seemed to be numerous jars of jellied cranberry sauce as well, along with a variety of jellies.

"Greg?" I called out again, but still no response.

Then, I turned around in the kitchen and, to my surprise and somewhat shock, saw tons of the cream pies, frosted cakes, and pastries I had baked over the last few days. They were set out on the two biggest counters next to my huge refrigerator, where I had stored them before they would be transported to the restaurant.

With a quizzical look on my face, I wondered why, in all hell, Greg would have taken all those cream pies, frosted cakes, and pastries out of my refrigerator. They weren't slated to be transported to the restaurant for another few days or so.

"GREG?" I called out very loudly this time as I stared at the array of my desserts on the two counters.

"GREG, why are all these pies, cakes, and pastries out of the refrigerator?" I called out, figuring the guy had to be in the bathroom.

I mean, where else could he have been?

To my further surprise and total incomprehension, I glanced into the far corner of my huge kitchen and saw a video camera mounted on a tripod, and if my eyes weren't deceiving me, I took in the fact that the video camera was turned onto the record mode, the little red light on top of the device the giveaway there.

I turned my attention momentarily away from the video camera because my anger began to intensify when I saw that my meringue pies had been taken out of the refrigerator as well.

"GREG, we need to put all this back in the refrigerator before it goes bad!" I called out. "The creams I use for these pies, cakes, and pastries are very delicate and run the risk of spoiling very quickly! And for just how long has all of this been out of the refrigerator? Greg, where are you, man? And what's up with the video camera? *What are you filming here, man?*"

"DAMN, even the chocolate mousse and meringue pie is out," I muttered as I undid the knot in my tie and left it dangling over my shirt now. "That can spoil even faster than the meringues..."

"Hey there, boss man," I heard, as Greg rounded the corner from where the bathroom was and sauntered into the kitchen to stand next to me at the first table covered in my baked desserts.

Greg, unlike me, was not wearing a suit and tie; rather, he was comfortably clad in a pair of beige cargo shorts, a black tee shirt with the word GAP written across the front of it, and dock shoes with no socks. It looked like the guy had really made himself comfortable before he had gotten to my place, his boss's place at that... I don't know about any of you out there, buds, but any time I'm in my boss's presence, even if it's in his home, even if I've done him a personal favor, I always dress appropriately in a suit and tie...and well-shined shoes at that. But at the moment, I didn't have time to worry about the fact that Greg, a gigantically muscular gym rat, blond, blue-eyed, and nearly six feet tall, was not appropriately dressed. No, I had other, more important things on my mind at that moment.

"Greg thanks for getting all the stuff you got from the stores. I appreciate it man, but why all the extra stuff I didn't ask for...and why, *why* are all these cakes and pies out of the refrigerator?" I asked him as he innocently picked up one of the cream pies. "And what's up with the video camera? I don't usually film myself when I'm working in the kitchen, bud... I mean, one time I had a film crew here from a cooking and food magazine, and that was filmed, but..."

"It's simple, boss man, simple as pie, as the saying goes," he said, giggled, and held the pie a tad higher, me not suspecting anything untoward.

"Simple how?" I asked, and without another word, Greg suddenly raised the pie to my face level and PIED me right in the face with it.

It made a sound like KERRRRSPLAAAAATTTT, sort of like in those old-time comedic movies when a character in the film got hit in the face with a pie...and I made a sound like, "AWWWWWWW, holy shit, HOLY FUCKING SHIT MAN! WHAT THE...*WHAT IN ALL HELL...*"

As I wriggled around a bit on my feet, Greg used the pie pan, whose pie was now all over my face, to smoosh and spread the creamy goo all over my face...

"GREG, GREG, WHAT THE FUCK MAN?" I roared after he let the pie pan drop to the floor, and I stood there with the ingredients of that pie all over my handsome face, dripping and splooching down onto my thousand-dollar suit.

"HEH, that's a good start, boss man," I heard Greg say as I used the first two fingers of both my hands to wipe the creamy mess away from my eyes... "I love the reaction of a guy after that first pie hits him in the face..."

"F-FIRST pie?" I reeled as I went on wiping the mess away from my eyes, but as soon as I was done doing that and I was able to see again, Greg pied me a second time with another of the gooey cream pies.

Once more, the sound of KERRRSPPLATTT filled the area as the pie connected with my puss.

"AWWWWWW, FUCCCCKKKK, FUCK, Greg, please!" I reeled, my arms flailing at my sides.

And as my arms flailed and confusion, not to mention humiliation, filled me, along with a feeling of definite rage now, Greg took that opportunity to pie me a third fucking time...right in the kisser, as the saying used to go in those old time comedic films I mentioned earlier...

Once more, the sound of KERRRSPPPFAATTT was heard...

"ERRRRRRRRRR!" was the sound I made that time, and from what I was able to taste, as I licked my lips, Greg had just hit me with a lemon meringue pie.

As I swallowed the lemon meringue, I realized, and quite stupidly at that, that I hadn't deciphered the flavors of the first two pies that Greg had pied and mottled me with.

And fuck of fucks, the residues from all three pies were dripping profusely now down onto my suit, my fucking thousand dollar suit at that...JEEEEZZZZZZ...

With my head lowered and looking down at the floor where the three empty pie pans now were and frantically trying to use all my fingers now to wipe the sludge off my face, I bellowed, "GREG, GREG, stop this shit, *stop it now*!" but instead of stopping I heard Greg say, "Coming up, one chocolate mousse cake for the boss man..."

Backing up with my head bent and still wiping the mess from my face, I pleaded, "NO, NO, not the chocolate mousse man...that's expensive and..."

But my pleas were rewarded with Greg smashing the mousse cake over the top of my bent-over head. The sounds of the cake being destroyed and the feeling of the cream, the goo, and the cake itself working into my well-coiffed, well-styled hair were maddening.

"SHIT, SHIT, SHIT!" I reeled crazily at this twisted turn of events.

Then, as the goop and mess from the three pies that Greg had splattered onto my face and the cake all over my head dripped down even more onto my suit, and now onto my shirt and undone tie as well, Greg helped it all along smearing it over the length of the front of my suit jacket, using the palms of his hands to really work it into the fabric...DAMN...

Backing up from my so-called work buddy, my feet slipping a bit in the mess that was also on the floor, I clenched my teeth and reeled loudly, "GREG, big and strong and mighty as you are, I will kick your sorry ass for this! AND HOLY FUCKING FUCKS, you're filming this! You're fucking filming this shit! This is what you set up the video camera for, man?"

I heard Greg chuckle and he picked up two pies and smashed them against the lower portion of the front of my suit jacket.

"Looking better and better, boss man," Greg laughed, and when I made the mistake of lifting my head to look at the guy and confront him, seeing as I had again wiped away the mess from my eyes, Greg pied me AGAIN in the face, this time with one of my blueberry pies...

KERRRSPFAATTTTT went the pie against my face, and Greg quickly, oh he was fast, he was FUCKING FAST, followed up by kersplatting me in the face with a cherry pie...one that had cream all over the top of it...

"AHHHHRRRRRR, Greg, you sick fuck," I sputtered around the mess of pie and cake in my mouth.

As I was again wiping the mess away from my eyes, my hands and fingers trembling now, I felt Greg smash some pies or cakes or whatever the fuck over the back of my suit jacket.

"AWWWWWW SHIITTTT, my suit...*my goddamned suit...*" I wailed miserably. "You're ruining my suit, Greg!"

"Just getting started, boss man," Greg said in a silly-sounding tone of voice. I could tell he was now standing a few feet from me...and the next thing I knew, the backs of my legs were hit with cream pies or cakes...FUCK...

I was too busy trying again to clear the mess from my eyes so I could see Greg and try to reason with him as to the why of why he was doing this to me....when my ass was pelted twice with, from the sound of it, the crusts of breaking up pies...

"AHHHHHHHRRRR, you bastard Greg," I cussed, REALLY slipping in the mess all over the floor now, bent doubled over now as well. "GREG, I-I can't balance man..."

"So much for kicking the gym rat's ass, huh bud?" Greg taunted me.

As I stood there, doubled over, my hands over my splatter-covered face, Greg began pouring something gooey, slimy, and soppy over the top of my head.

"WHAT...WHAT IN THE HELL!" I thundered crazily, the scent of whatever it was, sweet and sugary...mixing stickily with the mess of cake in my hair...and landing on the floor and smearing up my slip-on wingtips as well, making the floor even more slippery... FUCK!

I realized it was the Bosco chocolate syrup that Greg was pouring over my bent-over head...

"GREG, GREG, listen to me here, man, listen to me and stop this now!" I screamed. "I'm slipping, man...I'm gonna fall here...SHIIITTTT..."

For a few seconds, I didn't hear anything...and so I wiped the mess AGAIN from my eyes and managed to get myself to a straight-up standing position...but when I opened my eyes, there was Greg, standing a few feet away from me...AND to my woe, I saw that he was holding four, count 'em, FOUR of my cream pies, stacked up on top of each other in one of his hands...totally waiter style.

"Ready, boss man?" Greg asked me, grinning wickedly from ear to ear.

Stupidly thinking I could fend off the inevitable, I raised my hands and palms up and said, "NO GREG, NO, I'm not ready..."

...and I didn't dare try to back up too much, seeing as there was now, besides all the mess from my cakes and pies all over the floor, I was also standing in a huge puddle of Bosco chocolate syrup...and I didn't feel like slipping and falling...but at the same time, I didn't feel like being pied anymore...

With that, Greg wound back and hurled the four pies at me, getting me in the face each time...

KERSPLLATTTTT   KERPSPLAAATTTTT   KERSPLATTTTTT KERSPLATTTTTT was the comical yet sadistic sound the pies made as they covered and slopped my face some more, and as he did his dirty work, Greg laughed, laughing his head off...MY GOD!

As I stood there looking like a pied dude in an old-fashioned black-and-white comedy movie, I felt the fronts of my legs hit with pies and felt the mess dripping and sluicing down my suit pants and onto my slip-on wingtips, my five hundred dollar wingtips...SHIT!

"GREG, why, why, WHY?" I ranted as I, then, felt the guy grab the back collars of my suit jacket and shirt and pour a bottle of Mrs. Butterworth's syrup down there, soaking my back with the stuff.

"ARRRHHHHHHHHH...SHIIIITT, SHITTTTT, SHITTTTTT!" I squawked and found myself jumping dumbly from foot to foot in the mess I was standing in, helpless to stop the fucking guy from doing what he was doing to me, and as I jumped from foot to foot, I felt the mess on the floor sloshing around and finding its way into my shoes, ruining my navy blue nylon dress socks now.

"GREEEEEGGGGGG!" I squealed miserably as I felt Mrs. Butterworth's syrup dripping down my back under my button-down shirt and onto my boxer briefs underneath my suit pants.

When the bottle of Mrs. Butterworth's was empty, I stood there panting...and Greg meanly pied me three more times in the face. The sounds of KERRSPTAAAAATTTT were nearly insanity for me by then...

With a mouthful of pie, I tried to say Greg's name, but all that came out was a host of gibberish...and then I heard the sounds of eggs cracking.

"RFFFFFFFF..." I sputtered as I spit out the pie remnants and said, "OH NO, no, Greg...please..." Now, raw eggs began splattering over the top of my head, dripping down the sides of my face and under the collar of my button-down shirt.

I slipped and slid a few times in the mess. Greg instructed me to step out of my slip-on wingtips, which I instantly did, and then the bottoms of my dress socks were sodden in the mess on my kitchen floor... To be really sadistically funny, Greg grabbed me tight by my upper arms and slid me around and around in the gooey mess on the floor, really getting the bottoms of my dress socks messy now...

"GREG, GREG," I shouted miserably, feeling as if I were blindfolded by the mess of pie and cake all over my face. "What's the point of all this?"

"Comedy, Nash, lighthearted comedy," Greg replied as he held me tighter by my upper arms and slid me around more in the mess on the floor.

"GOD!" was all I could say then, *oh God*, then Greg had lined up three cream pies on the counter, the chocolate mousse pie in the center. Holding me now by one arm, Greg grabbed my mussed-up, gooey mess of hair and pushed my face down, down, *and down* into the first cream pie.

"PWUHHHHHHHHHH..." was the sound I made as my handsome puss connected with the pie, Greg laughing crazily by then.

Holding me tight by my arm and hair, Greg moved me to the last pie on the counter, giggled like a sadistic school kid, said, "And here we go again," and repeated the action, plunging my face down into it.

"And now for the crème de la crème of these three pies," Greg stated in a sing-song tone of voice and pushed my face down into the cream and chocolate mousse pie, this time really grinding my face into it.

"RRRRRRRRRRRRHHHHH..." I raged with incomprehensible anger.

I made the mistake of trying to pull out of Greg's firm, strong grasp, and all I got for my efforts was to go slip-sliding around and around in the mess all over the floor.

"WHOA, WHOA, WHOA!" I bellowed as I danced in my socks and totally by then ruined suit and tie in the goo... "Some fucking lighthearted comedy this is, Greg! This isn't funny, not funny what-so-fucking-ever so-called bud of mine!"

Greg laughed as he watched me dancing around in the gooey mess on the floor, my arms flapping uselessly and crazily at my sides...and to add insult to my misery, Greg picked up a few eggs and threw them down at my socked feet, so now I was dancing in egg yolk and on eggshells, which I have to say really smarted through my goo covered dress socks...

"I'm gonna fall, I'm gonna fall, I'm gonna fall," I said loudly as I went on sliding in the mess, at the same time trying to use my fingers to clean the mess from my eyes...but that was nearly impossible at that point...seeing as my fingers were sodden with cream, meringue, and syrup, so really, all I was doing was adding to my face what was already there.

"I'm gonna fall, I'm gonna fall, *I'm gonna fall*," Greg meanly mimicked me. "That sounds like the makings for a good rap song, boss man..."

"HA, HA, HA, so funny you are, Greg," I snarled and managed to grab onto the end of one of the counters where Greg had set out all my cakes, cream pies, pastries, and other baked creations.

Holding onto the counter edge, I managed to balance myself on my slopped-up socked feet, panting, gasping, and looking like a mess...looking beyond a mess, actually...

Then, holding onto the counter edge with two hands, my head hanging down and all the sludge dripping all over me, I croaked out, "Greg, why are you doing this to me? And even more, why in all fucks are you filming this?"

In response to my question, Greg opened one of the canned soups by pulling the tab back on it. He stepped over to me, and without any hesitation, he undid the zipper on my suit pants.

"GREG, NO, NO, what now, man?" I panted, holding onto the counter edge tight.

Greg poured the contents of the soup can, minestrone to be exact, down my open fly opening.

"AGGGGHHHHHHH...." I sniveled loudly as I felt the soup dripping down my legs under my suit pants. It seemed as if I hoisted myself to my socked tiptoes...and did a senseless-looking sexy dance.

"And now for the back side, boss man," Greg said after the soup can was empty.

"What do you mean?" I asked incredulously, horrorstruck over all of this.

And just like that, Greg responded to my question, which made me wish I hadn't asked...because he yanked my suit pants back using my belt as a handle, exposing my white boxer briefs, and poured a can of green split pea soup down them back there.

"AHHHHHHHHHHHHH! OH THE SHAME!" I cried miserably and swiveled even more on my socked-tip toes, "Split pea in the back and minestrone in the front. What a fucked up soup concoction..."

"Spoken like the top-chef you are, boss man," Greg snickered.

"FUCK, so glad you approve," I responded in a snarky tone of voice.

"Now stay up on those sexy socked toes of yours, boss man," Greg said to me in a commanding tone of voice.

"And for what reason, may I ask?" I reeled back at the guy, as he squeezed my legs back and front so that the soups he'd poured down my legs front and back would drip into my already ruined suit pants.

"You'll find out momentarily," Greg chuckled, and the next thing I knew he was throwing eggs at the bottoms of my upturned feet.

"OWWWWWW!" I bellowed as the eggs cracked against my soles, and I felt the yolk dripping down the bottoms of my socks.

I leaned my head down and sniveled and whimpered miserably, snorting loudly through my nose, seeing as some of the mess of cream all over my face had found its way up my damned nostrils.

After Greg felt he had pelted the bottoms of my socked feet enough with eggs, he opened a bottle of soy sauce and spread half of it all over the sections of my kitchen floor that hadn't yet been soiled with food and goo mess. The rest of the soy sauce the fucking jokester poured down the open section of the front of my shirt, soaking my chest and stomach areas with soy sauce...GOD!

"GREG!" I reeled in his face, even though I really couldn't see his face at the moment. "When is this going to stop? Look at what you've done to me and my kitchen, for God's sake, man!"

"Eventually, boss man, but not right now," Greg replied and once more grabbed my upper arms in a firm grasp. "For now, it's time for you to go slipping and sliding again. Let's see how well you do on your egg-slopped nylon socked feety bottoms..."

Saying that, he pulled me away from the counter edge I had been grasping to keep my damned balance.

"OH NO, No, Greg, Please!" I wailed as the guy pushed me forward in the soy sauce and gooey mess all over my kitchen floor, "...my egg slopped nylon socked feety bottoms indeed...oh holy fucks, Greg!"

And as he had predicted, I slipped round and round like a fool on my egg-splattered feet bottoms.

"ARRHHHHHH, GREG, I'm gonna fall, I'm gonna fall, I'm gonna fall!" I shouted as I slid and slipped and slipped and slipped and slid.

"There's that rap again," Greg chided me from where he was standing by the counter.

"Not funny, man. *None of this is funny!*" I protested wildly as I slid around in the muck.

"What say we make it just a tad more challenging?" Greg asked.

My eyes went wide open. I stupidly turned toward him; what in hell did he mean? Seeing as I felt I was presently being challenged enough, thank you, and this time, I got pied again, three times, right in the face... KERSPLAATTTT KERSPLLATTTTTT KERSPLATTTTTT.

"AWWWWWW!" I cried out, put my hands over my face, and as I slid some more in the muck, it finally happened. I fell to the floor, landing unceremoniously on my sexy tush...JEEEEZZZZ...with my soggy socked feeties, as Greg had called them, pointing straight up for a moment...till he grabbed both of them by the ankles...

He meanly dragged me across the soy-sauced kitchen floor by my raised socked ankles, mussing up the back of my suit jacket and white shirt all the more...and over to the second counter where all the cakes and pies and pastries he hadn't used on me still were...FUCK! Just as the guy reached down to hoist me off the floor and into his arms, I didn't need three guesses to know what the fucking fuck he was about to do. He held me aloft for the moment. He was getting some of the mess that was all over me on himself. Obviously, he didn't give a rat's ass. Now I knew why the fucker had changed out of his own suit and tie...and then he lifted me higher over the second counter that was covered with my baked desserts...

"GREG, put me down, you louse!" I said in a demanding tone but soon realized that I made a mistake. Because he dropped me bodily...atop the counter of cakes, cream pies, and pastries... "AWWWWWW...SHHHHIIITTT man..."

"And now round and round we go, Nash ol' boy," Greg chided me laughingly, grabbed my calves, and rolled me round and round, just as he had just said in the mess of cakes, cream pies, and pastries...

"FUCK, FUCK, FUCK," I said helplessly.

"Oh man, what a gunge epic this will be, Nash," Greg said.

"G-GUNGE?" I asked as he stepped over to my head and pressed my face into a red velvet creamy pastry and then into a creamy Napoleon pastry. "What in all hell is gunge? You twisted fuck!" I screamed.

"Exactly what I'm doing to you, boss man, gunging you..." Greg replied, sounding oh so reasonable, as if what he was subjecting me to was perfectly normal for two guys to be engaging in, and then sploshed my face into a cannoli cream pastry. "And believe me, boss man; the video I'm making here today will garner me thousands, maybe even millions of dollars!"

"You can't be serious!" I railed, as the guy began rolling me back and forth atop the counter in the creamy, crusty, and sugary mess...

After he had rolled me back and forth for what seemed like umpteen times in the cakes, cream pies, and pastries on the second counter, Greg left me stretched out on my stomach with my socked, messy feet dangling off the end of the counter...and he proceeded to rub the cream from some of the cream pies into my socks, running his hands up my calves under my suit pants...

...and lo and fucking behold, I realized at that moment that my cock was rock hard in my gunged (a word I had just learned the meaning of) suit pants and boxer briefs. What was up with that? I ask you, buds?

When Greg was done rubbing a good amount of cream all over my damned socks, he turned me over on my back atop the counter and positioned me straight out with my arms at my sides and my legs together. When I reached up to wipe the mess away from my eyes, Greg pied me twice more in the face.

I got the message and left my arms at my sides; a feeling of total helplessness had enveloped me, and yet my cock was rage-hard. I was sure that Greg saw the bulge in my most ruined suit pants...

THEN, oh fuck, THEN, as I lay there feeling like a sacrificial lamb of sorts, the fucking guy started seasoning me, at least it seemed so...

Standing next to me and working fast, Greg opened various jars of the jellies he had bought.

With my head raised a bit and able to see through a blur what he was doing, I muttered the words, "Oh fuck..." and laid my head back down. Greg was pouring mint, grape, peach, and other flavors of jelly all over me, from my neck down to my chest area, to my crotch, all over my pants legs, and finally, he used marmalade to coat my socked feet with...

I lay there whimpering miserably, smelling real sweet from all the sugary crap he had me covered in, along with smelling sour from the damned soy sauce the guy had, in a way, sautéed me in...GOD!

"And now for the flipside, boss man," Greg said and showing his brute strength, he flipped me over on the counter onto my stomach...

And the next thing I knew, he was pouring jar after jar after jar of tomato sauce over me, from the back of my head to the back of my suit jacket, down my pants legs, finishing it off by sopping it over my socks...

When the guy was done, I felt that I didn't even look human anymore... FUCKKKK, I was beyond pied and gunged...

All the jars of tomato sauce were empty. Now Greg grabbed me by the back collars of my totally ruined suit jacket and shirt and hauled me upwards...

"ACCCHHHHH..." I screeched as he dragged me off the countertop. "WH-whatttt, now you sick prankster?"

"Almost done, BOSSS MAAAN, almost finally finished," Greg said with a hint of sarcasm to his tone. He held me by the back collars of my suit jacket and shirt and slip-slid me over to one of my kitchen chairs, plopped me down in it, pushed my head down so I was staring at the floor...and began splooshing bottles of ketchup over the top of my head.

"AWWWWWW FUCK, FUCK, FUCKKKKKK..." I complained.

"End of the epic, boss man," Greg laughed when the last bottle of ketchup was empty.

With the redness of ketchup dripping down all over what was already in my hair and on my face, I clenched my teeth and was literally speechless at that point...not to mention the fact that my cock was now beyond rage hard in my completely ruined suit pants and boxer briefs...

"I hope you have a good cleaning lady, boss man," Greg laughed and pushed me off the chair, causing me to land on my hands and knees in the mess all over the kitchen floor.

"So funny you are, ASSSHOLE," I slurred through trembling lips.

As I slowly got myself to my messy, socked feet, I heard the sounds of Greg packing something up...

"WH-whatttt the fuck are you doing now." I could not stop the tremble in my voice. I asked as I got to my feet...and FINALLY wiped the mess away from my eyes...

I saw that Greg had packed up his video camera and tripod and was holding one last cream pie in his hand.

"I'll be on my way now, boss man; I'll leave you to clean up the mess..." Greg laughed and threw the pie at me, hitting his target, *my face, head-on.*

"AWWWWWWWW..." I roared and fell backward, landing on my ass and then splayed out on my back on my mussed-up kitchen floor...

As I lay there panting, I heard Greg let himself out of my apartment...

"SHIT, SHIT, SHIT, pied and gunged," I said silently...and then...*then*, to my utter disbelief, I reached one hand down to my crotch, extracted my erection from my boxer briefs, and began stroking...using the cream and other mess all over me as a lubricant...

"Yeah, gonna really gunge now..." I said with a sick-looking grin, wanting my cum to mix with the mess all over me, which would be real gourmet gunge for a gourmet chef like me.

/The End/

Archie and his Neighbor, Mr. Matthews

IT WAS 8:00 AM when Mike Matthews' doorbell rang, right when the 40-year-old finance executive was about to complete his morning workout in his state-of-the-art gym in the basement of his house.

As he dashed up the basement steps, clad in a pair of tight-fitting red gym shorts, ankle-length black sweat socks, and black sneakers with a towel draped around his bull-sized neck, Mike Matthews muttered to himself, "Now, who the hell could that be so early on a damned Saturday morning?"

When he reached the front door and opened it, he saw his son's best friend, Archie, or, as he called him, Carrot Top, because of his flaming red hair, standing there.

Panting a bit, the finance executive said, "Hey there, good morning, Carrot Top. What brings you here so early on a Saturday morning?"

"Well, good morning to you too Mr. Matthews, I'm uh, I'm here to pick Warren up, remember?" Archie, a college freshman said, as he suddenly found himself taking in the sight...

...and the sweaty, salty scent of his best friend's father...

...as the man's colossally-sized chest seemed to be heaving up and down a bit with each breath he took.

Running a huge, paw-sized hand through his sweat-sopped, corporately styled dark hair, Mike Matthews said, "Pick Warren up for what?" Not noticing that his son's friend seemed to be wallowing in the sight of his deep and hairy...and extremely smelly armpit...

"Uh, we're going camping for the long weekend," Archie replied while trying to focus on the conversation. "My uncle has a cabin upstate and..."

Wiping the back of his big neck and huge chest a bit with the towel that had been hanging around his neck, Mr. Matthews cut Archie off in mid-sentence. He then added, "Well, I'm sorry to tell you that you and Warren must have gotten your signals crossed,

Carrot Top, because he and my wife left last night to spend the long weekend with her sister and her sister's husband, and, yes, Warren's cousins."

A look of confusion came over Archie's face as he said, "Are you kidding me, Mr. Matthews? Because you see, Warren and I made the camping trip plans weeks ago."

"Nope, not kidding, Carrot Top. He went with my wife to her sister's and his cousins," the finance executive said, re-draping his towel around the back of his neck and adjusting his shoulders. "The only reason I didn't go with them is because I have a lot of office work I brought home with me to do. No long weekend for me."

"Yeah, I suppose not," Archie said, sounding totally dejected. "But it sure looks like you got to work out at least..."

"Yeah, I sure did at that," Mike Matthews said to Archie. "Say, did Warren ever show you my totally state-of-the-art gym down in the basement?" he asked in an inquisitive tone.

"No, he didn't, Mr. Matthews," Archie responded.

"Well, seeing as it looks like you're not going camping, why don't I show it to you?" Mr. Matthews suggested. "I'll even tell Warren to let you use it once in a while. You can call him on his cell after you see the gym, plus you two can figure out where you got your signals crossed about going camping."

Stepping into the house, Archie said, "Yeah, that would be great, Mr. Matthews, thanks..."

After closing and locking the front door, Mr. Matthews said, "Follow me, Carrot Top."

"Sure thing," Archie replied, and as he followed the well-built older man through the living room, he couldn't keep his eyes off how Mr. Matthews' rock-hard, coconut-shaped ass globes filled out the back of his tight red gym shorts...

...and the fact that they were totally sweat-soaked...

"Sorry about my appearance, by the way, Carrot Top," the finance executive said as he approached the basement stairs in the kitchen. "But you obviously caught me in the middle of finishing up my morning workout..."

"Yeah, I uh, I can tell," Archie said to the well-toned man's ripped and muscular back. "It looks like you really like punishing yourself through a hard and grueling workout..."

As they headed down the steps to the basement/gym, Mike said, "Yeah, I do love working myself over real hard with weights before I get to my corporate work... It really clears my head..." he completed...

...and then turned to face his son's friend...

"Makes me feel all pumped up..." Mr. Matthews said...

...as Archie swallowed hard at the sight of the man's amazing musculature...

"Yeah! Pumped up is right. Mr. Matthews," Archie said, without realizing that he was taking shaky steps toward the sweaty, worked-out, hard muscled finance executive.

"Especially around here...on your nips...Mr. Matthews..." Archie said and squeezed his best friend's dad's right-sided nipple...HARD...

"HUHHHHHHHHH! Holy shit, Carrot Top!" Mike suddenly swooned. "JEEZ KID, take it easy there. I got real sensitive nips for a guy!"

But, instead of letting go of Mr. Matthew's nips, and as if he were in a trance, Archie reached with his other hand and grabbed the finance executive's left-sided nipple...

"HOOOOOOOOO, holy fucks, Carrot Top, what's up with you? Got a thing for a man's jutted-up nips or something?" Mike panted and tottered stupidly on his feet...

...as Archie applied intense pressure and twisted his best friend's dad's nipples as if they were bottle caps...

He, then, yanked forward on Mr. Matthews' nipples, still squeezing the hyper-sensitive nubs and twisting them harder yet...

"AWWWWHHHHH GAWD! C'mon, Carrot Top, leggo of my damned tits! The finance executive demanded...

...and found himself then standing nearly nose to nose, or, if you prefer, mouth to mouth with his son's best friend...

"L-leggo...my...tits...Carrot Top..." the finance executive whispered...

...and, as he whispered, he found that his trembling lips were grazing Archie's...

"Mr. Matthews, you outweigh and outmuscle me more than a few pounds over," Archie whispered, his lips grazing the older man's as well...

...and squeezed the finance executive's nipples harder yet, twisting the bejesus out of them at that point...

"If you want me to let go of your nipples so badly you could swat me off them as if I were a fly," Archie whispered, pecking the man's lips a bit at the same time.

"HUUUHHHHHH! *Fucking Carrot Top...*" Mike seethed crazily, as Archie's lips grazed his even more. "This is what gets you off, kid? This is what you like? Playing with your best bud's dad's pumped-up man-sized tits? *JEEEEZZZZZ man...*"

To add to Mr. Matthews' shock (or perhaps not), Archie let go of his nipples, hunkered down a bit, and slurped his best friend's dad's right-sided nipple into his mouth.

"AWWWWWHHHHH FUCKS, you crazy carrot-topped kid!" Mr. Matthews sputtered through clenched teeth...

...as Archie quickly began sucking, licking, and chewing on his big erect nub...

"HUHHHHH! What a twisted game Carrot Top, overpower a man via his tits, his MAN tits!" the finance executive snarled, tottering a bit and unbalanced on his sneaker-clad feet...

...as Archie sucked his nipple harder...

...and then reached down to grip one of the man's rock-hard ass cheeks...

"HUHHHHHHH fucking fucks, Carrot Top, I get the feeling you don't give a rat's ass that Warren left you high and dry!" Mr. Matthews sputtered.

Gripping his friend's dad's both ass cheeks now tighter through his gym shorts; Archie stopped sucking Mr. Matthews' right-sided nipple. He looked up and said, "Yeah, more like it's you who he left high and dry, Mr. Matthews," and then quickly gobbled the finance executive's left-sided nipple into what felt to the man like a very greedy, very hungry mouth...

"FFFFFFUUUCCCKKK, yeah, left me high and dry AND easy pickings for you, Carrot Top," Mike panted...

...and then...

Now, Archie felt the man's huge hands running over the top of his head, pressing his face against his chest, allowing the college freshman to get more of that nipple into his mouth...

"Yeah, that's it, Carrot Top. Work my nips, *fucking work my nips, kid...*" the finance executive crooned, and Archie felt elated as a longtime fantasy of his had seemed to finally have been realized.

As he worked his best friend's dad's nipples alternately in and out of his mouth, Archie gripped the sides of the man's gym shorts and pulled...HARD...shredding the shorts off the finance executive...

"HUHHHHHH, think I know what you want next, Carrot Top," Mike Matthews grunted as he pressed himself harder against his son's best buddy. Archie felt the erection pressing against him that he knew had been in those gym shorts all along.

The college freshman stopped working the man's now beyond jutted-up nipples, held tight to his upper arms, looked down at the massive girth between his best friend's dad's legs, swallowed hard, and panted, "Mr. Matthews, you have no idea what I want next... what I've wanted next for so long...nice to see you were commando under your gym shorts..."

And with that, Archie shucked off his pullover polo shirt as Mr. Matthews began undoing the belt on the carrot-topped young man's jeans...

...And shortly, the finance executive found himself propped up atop one of his workout benches, on his back, wearing just his black ankle-length sweat socks and black sneakers...

...as naked Carrot topped Archie lay atop him and was hungrily and ravenously kissing his lips, he snaked his tongue into his best friend's dad's mouth and sucked hard on the man's tongue...

Archie then ran his fingers through the man's hair and kissed him more and more on the mouth, causing Mike Matthews to feel as if he were being devoured...

When he stopped for air, Mr. Matthews, up on his elbows, grinned up at the college freshman and, in a snarky and sexy-sounding tone of voice, asked, "Tell me, Carrot Top, how long have you harbored these feelings for me, huh?"

Smiling devilishly, Archie kissed Mr. Matthews on the cheek and said, "Let's say I've been crushing on you since I was a kid, Mr. Matthews..."

Still hunkered up on his elbows, the finance executive watched as his son's best friend began inching his way downward. When Archie hoisted the man's tree-trunk-like legs upwards with his black sweat-socked ankles, Mike Matthews didn't need three guesses to know what the college freshman planned to do to him next...

Using his own pre cum as a lube and the sweaty walls of the finance executive's hole, Archie began sliding his erection into the man's hole, inch by loving inch...

"AWWWWWWWW GOD, Carrot Top, fucking my damned shit chute now!" Mike Matthews thundered and gripped the sides of the workout bench he lay on super-tight. "AWWWWWW YEAH never knew this could feel so fucking amazing, having a dude's cock up my ass, fucking COCK UP MY ASSSSSS!"

Holding tight to the man's sweat-socked ankles, Archie began a rhythmic fucking motion as he plowed in and out of his best friend's dad's hole...

"FUCCCKKK Carrot Top, you really opened my eyes...and my nips and my hole at that, to a lot of new sensations today!" the finance executive exclaimed. "DAMN, kid! Fuck me harder, that cock up my ass feels amazing, COCK UP MY ASS!"

As he thrust in and out of the man's hole, as the sounds of squishing erotically filled the air, Archie panted, "Gimmie... Gimmie.... time Mr. Matthews, I'll introduce you... and open your eyes to... sensations you NEVER knew before...FFFUCK, I'm gonna cum soon, you handsome fuck!"

"Oh fuck yeah; I can actually feel your flagpole throbbing inside me, Carrot Top!" Mike thundered, reached down, and grabbed his own throbbing erection...

...and as Archie began spurting his thick creamy mess into his best friend's dad's hole, the finance executive stroked a Wall Street-sized load from himself...

The sounds of the two men grunting, gasping, and roaring as they shot their loads in unison filled the basement/gym...

With one hand, Mr. Matthews stroked and choked his cock till every last drop of his cum was spent, and with his other hand, he stroked Archie's flaming red hair...

"Fucking Carrot Top, *fucking hot Carrot Top,* fucking my ass, got your goddamned cock up my ass...cock up my ass, of all things..." the finance executive exclaimed, practically crying tears of joy at that point.

When Archie was spent, he let his deflating cock slip from the older man's hole, hunched himself upwards, and kissed his best friend's dad's nipples a few times each... sucking the man's cum off them...

...as the finance executive continued running his fingers through Archie's red hair...

Then, the carrot-topped college freshman said to his best friend's dad, "Now, Mr. Matthews, tell me, how you feel about bondage games?"

Mike Matthews' jaw dropped, and his spent cock tingled...

/To Be Continued.../

Archie and his Neighbor, Mr. Matthews 2

IT WAS NOW 11:00 AM OF WHAT MIKE MATTHEWS, Finance Executive, would have called a fateful Saturday morning, and three hours since the man's son's best friend, Archie, whom the finance executive called Carrot Top, because of his flaming red hair, had shown up at his house...

...and did things to him that at the age of 40, married to the same woman since he was 20 years old and with a son headed off to college, he never could have fathomed... (or perhaps he could have fathomed?)

.....overpowered by his sensitive nipples, DAMN, once that carrot-topped kid had had him by the nips, he was like putty in his hands...squeezing and twisting his jutted-up tits, his MAN TITS, as if they were bottle caps, causing the finance executive to feel things in his loins he'd never felt before (or did he?). His damned nipples were on total display and just asking for it because he had just finished his morning workout, shirtless, in his private basement/gym, and when he demanded the kid let go of his damned nipples, well, instead of obeying orders, the carrot-topped mother fucker went to work sucking his hard tits, his MAN TITS, FUCK...sucking his nipples, chewing on them like they were the best-tasting things on God's green earth...AND, and holding him tight by his muscular ass globes as he feasted like a beast on those damned nipples...MAN TITS, DAMN!! And when his son's buddy kissed and devoured him at the mouth...well, all of that was totally incredible... but then, when the dude tore his gym shorts off him and found him commando under them, he slid his cock into his anal canal...FUCKKKK! He felt A LOT OF THINGS... It seemed to the finance executive that his goddamned hole had literally sucked that college freshman's cock inside him. For Mike Matthews, in his pain and ecstasy, it was all just too over the top. BECAUSE..... *because* he wanted Carrot Top's cock deep, deeper inside him with each thrust the kid made as he plowed him, MY GOD...and then to cum the way he did as that kid fucked him six ways to Sunday...

And even though he outweighed and outmuscled the carrot-topped college freshman by beyond God knows how many pounds, not once, not fucking once, did he attempt to shoo the kid away...

...if anything, he seemed to want more and more AND MORE of what his son's best buddy was doing to him...

And then, MY GOD, the cum was amazing... Never before...NEVER before in his 40 years did he cum like that, not even with his wife, DAMN! And the feeling of his son's best friend's splooge flooding his hole, coating his ass walls, it was like total fucking bliss...

The cherry on top was carrot top, revealing that he had been crushing on him since he was a kid?

Well, he supposed it was better, somewhat better than if his son's best buddy had a thing for his wife that would never have gone well at all for the finance executive. HA, Mr. Matthews thought, better the kid fuck my ass than my wife's pussy. What a twisted thought!

Three goddamned hours now since it had happened, and instead of feeling spent and all used up, the finance executive wanted more...

MORE...and MORE.....

...and lo and fucking behold, the ol' carrot topped college freshman was giving him just that...MORE...

Because now, seeing as Mike Matthews' son's best friend had teasingly asked him how he felt about bondage games, the well-toned, built-like-a-brick shit house finance executive found himself bound with his wrists above his head, with a jump-rope that he used for his workouts, that Archie had found on the floor of the man's basement gym, towards the bed board of his and his wife's bed upstairs in their bedroom...stretched out on his ripped muscular back...for the moment...his sneakers having been taken off his gigantic smelly feet, wearing just his ankle-length black sweat socks...

...and grunting in a mixture of misery and ecstasy, as the carrot topped college boy used more of his jump ropes to secure his socked ankles to the sides of the bed board...

...literally practically folding the muscleman in half on his and his wife's bed...

"HUHHHHHH, JEEZ Carrot Top, when you asked me how I felt about bondage games, I didn't for a goddamned second think that this was what you had in mind," Mike Matthews seethed, his head resting on his muscular pulled up above his arms, looking up and watching as Archie tied his sweat-socked ankles securely to the sides of the bed board.

"As I told you, Mr. Matthews, I plan to introduce you to things you've never imagined," Archie chuckled and kissed the finance executive's socked foot that he had just finished tying to the bed board. "Damn, your feet really stink..."

As Archie got to work binding the man's other foot up to the bed board, the finance executive said, in a snarky tone, "Damnnn kid, I had worked out and sweated in those socks for more than two hours before you surprised me by showing up here today...you really think those socks of mine are gonna smell like they just came out of the clothes dryer?"

"Good point, Mr. Matthews," Archie said, also sounding snarky and like with the finance executive's first sweat-socked foot, when he was done tying it to the bed board, he gave it a kiss.

"So that's why you tied me up like this kid, all folded in half so you could kiss my smelly sweat socks?" Mr. Matthews asked most sarcastically.

Grinning down at his prize, Archie said, "Not quite Mr. Matthews..." He moved down to the bound finance executive's ass on display...and his ass hole...

...the man's gaping hole, which was practically looking up at the bedroom ceiling...

"JEEZ kid, look at this shit now. You got me tied up here and spread out like a Thanksgiving turkey. Not to mention that I'm at full mast in my cock all over again, can't get over that," Mr. Matthews panted, curling his toes back and forth under his stinky sweat socks as he spoke. "Look at me! Just fucking look at me, forty years old, just shot a whopper of a load not that long ago, and I'm all hard in the cock again...and shot my load because your cock was up my ass at that...goddamned carrot top you are...now it seems like I'm getting all chubbed up in the cock from you tyin' me the fuck up like this...JEEZ..."

As Archie settled himself at Mr. Matthews' upturned ass cheeks, he gave them a quick swat and said, "I will say this, Mr. Matthews, for a man who makes his living in a suit and tie behind a desk on Wall Street, you certainly have a way with words, you should have maybe been a writer instead of a finance executive...what do you think?"

The finance executive licked his lips and said, "At this very moment, I think what I really think doesn't matter much to you...so, now that you got me all bound up for your bondage games, as you called them, what's next? Gonna cock up my ass again?"

"HEH, not just yet, Mr. Matthews. I think I'll make you wait a bit for that," Archie said, sounding sinister as hell at that point. "Making you wait is called edging..."

"So I'm just to lie here all bound up in my goddamned smelly sweat socks and chitter chatter with you and..." the finance executive sputtered, but his words were cut short when Archie grabbed his ass cheeks hard, spread them as wide as possible and spit into his hole...numerous times...

"HUUHHHHH, WH-what the fuck, Carrot Top?" Mr. Matthews fumed, his massive chest heaving up and down. "Using my damned anal canal as a goddamned spittoon?"

After spitting a few more times into the man's sweaty, musty, and still cum sopped hole, Archie leaned down, stuck out his tongue...

...and began flicking the tip of it around and around in the finance executive's anal canal, as the man had so aptly called it just seconds ago...

"AWWWWWWWHHHH FUUUCCCKK, FUCKING FUCKS!" Mike Matthews suddenly thundered. "Oh my God, Carrot Top, oh my fucking God, you-you're fucking tonguing and rimming my hole, oh my fucks, NEVER, never before in my forty years... AWWWWWWWHHH GAWWWDDDD!"

To tantalize and tease his prize all the more, Archie dribbled liberally into Mr. Matthews' hole, gripped his ass cheeks tighter yet...

...and began sucking his ass walls, gulping back his saliva and his cum, whatever residue there was of it, from earlier...

"HUUUUHHHHH, Y-you're making me crazy here, Carrot Top!" the finance executive croaked throatily.

In response to his moaning and panting, Archie swirled his tongue round and round and round against Mike Matthews' rosebud.

"EERRRRRRRHHH, GAWWD..." was the finance executive's response. "MY, my goddamned cock is pounding like a jackhammer, you crazy kid!"

Pausing for a moment in his ass-work, Archie looked up into the man's face of shock and gleefully said, "Yeah and all because I'm treating your manhole like it was a pussy hole..."

"HA, HA, HA for me, Carrot Top, that's one hundred percent man ass beef you're eating back there, or down there, whatever the fucking fucks you prefer," Mr. Matthews ranted. "Fuck, look at me here, fucking tied up in my sweat socks and my asshole bein' eaten by my son's best friend..."

"Yeah, it doesn't get much better than this, eh, Mr. Matthews?" Archie chided the man and slid his tongue tip into the man's now saturated ass lips.

"HUHHHHHHH, this is torture, Carrot Top, fucking exquisite torture, but torture none-the-fucking-less...GAWWWDDDD..." the finance executive cried out then.

Archie then began a series of continuous ministrations of dribbling, spitting, flicking his tongue, sucking the man's ass walls, and teasing Mr. Matthews' rosebud with his tongue, lips, and mouth.

The finance executive's muscular body broke out in wild goosebumps, and tears of both joy and madness filled his big dark eyes...

...as Archie worked his asshole mouth-wise, AND, as if he would never stop...

"GOD, my cock is so hard it's painful, Carrot Top, and I can feel it oozing pre cum," Mr. Matthews stated breathlessly... "No wonder you wanted me tied the fuck up this way, no way for me to get to my stalk...*edging me is right like you said...*"

Archie giggled fiendishly, and Mr. Matthews felt the college freshman handling his tight and cum-filled testicles, pulling them toward himself...pulling them toward his mouth...

"HOOOO GOD, what now, kid, *what the fuck now?*" the finance executive demanded. "As if I had any say in the matter, that is..JEEZ..."

Mike Matthews received his reply from Archie a few seconds later...

...as the kid held his testicles tight between his thumb and index finger...

...and began slathering his tongue now over and over those tight cum filled balls...

"HHHHHUUUUNNNN, you know Carrot Top, I gotta tell you here, you really know how to treat a guy!" the finance executive said breathlessly...and joyfully. "GAWWWD, you're goin' places my wife never did..."

As he held the man's testicles tighter, Archie stopped licking them for a moment, said, "No shit Sherlock," and then, to Mr. Mike Matthews' shock of shocks, the college freshman slurped one of his tender testicles into his mouth...

...and sucked the fuck out of it...

"ARRRRHHHHH! Fucking fucks Carrot Top, sucking my balls now?" the finance executive rasped crazily. "Not sure if I'm loving or hating that, you lunatic kid... FUCCKK..."

Mike Matthews arched his head a bit forward to watch as Archie sucked his testicles alternately in and out of his mouth, chills coursing through his muscular goose-bumped body...his mouth let out a whiff, and he threw his head back again.

"MY GOD, Carrot Top, if anyone had told me when I woke up today that this would happen after my work out and this is how I would be spending my morning, I never would have believed it. Being feasted on by my kid's best friend...of all things...DAMN!!" the finance executive blubbered at that point.

Pausing again in his mouth action, holding Mr. Matthews' saliva-soaked sort of swollen balls in his hand, Archie giggled and said, "Your morning, Mr. Matthews? Your morning? I have a newsflash for you, I'm going to be spending more than just the morning here with you today..."

And with that, Archie resumed sucking the finance executive's testicles in and out of his, what Mr. Mike Matthews had come to call his greedy hungry mouth...

The sounds of his testicles being slurped and sucked on filled the bedroom. The air was now thick with Archie's slurps and Mr. Matthew's heat. The finance executive muttered "Looks like no office work after all for me today...*fucking Carrot Cop!*"

"MMMMMMMM..." Archie crooned as he gently chewed next on his best friend's dad's testicles...

"HUHHHHHH, hey kid, easy with my balls, huh?" Mr. Matthews asked with a sexy-as-all-hell sneer on his face. "I might want to make my son Warren a big brother at some point, HA! Kidding kid, fucking kidding..."

After a good while, Mr. Mike Matthews' testicles had been sucked up to the size of two kiwis in his sweaty saliva-soaked sac. The man was panting breathlessly, his huge muscular torso heaving up and down on the bed in his bound-up folded position...

"Fucking Carrot Top, because of everything you've subjected me to here, every part of my body feels alive and tingling..." the finance executive muttered and lay still as Archie began quickly undoing the ropes holding him to the bed board, the redheaded college freshman's cock as tall as the Empire State Building as well at that point...

A few short moments later, like earlier, Archie hoisted the man's rectum into position, aimed his erect cock at it, and slid his cock home, slowly, inch by inch, the way he had quickly come to learn that the finance executive loved it...

"AWWWWWWHHH, yes! Oh, for the love of God and all the angels, Carrot Top, cock up my ass, that's it, kid, cock up my ass!" Mr. Mike Matthews demanded crazily, running his fingers lovingly through Archie's red hair, stroking the back of the kid's neck. "Yeah, Carrot Top, *cock up my ass...*"

As Archie began fucking the man for the second time that morning, the finance executive also repeated his earlier action. He reached down, grabbed his throbbing erection...

...and as his son's best friend speared him like crazy, he began stroking his manhood...

"Oh, yeah Carrot Top, what a pair we are, huh? Who would've thought it?" Mike Matthews gurgled. "GOD, I feel like I'm gonna cum as potently as I did earlier, kid! That's the sleazy effect you've had on me here today...AWWWWW FUCK, cock up my ass, and that feels electric!"

As Archie thrust in and out of the finance executive's hole for the second time that morning, he felt himself preparing to fill the man's opening with what he knew as well would be a whopper of a second load...

Soon, both were roaring in a man's passion as they each shot their loads for the second time that morning, Archie, filling his best friend's dad's anal canal with his college freshman spunk, and Mike Matthews spurting his executive mess all over his colossally built upper torso.

As Archie seemed to cum and cum like a madman inside his best friend's dad's hole, he smacked the man's ass cheeks hard, gripped, and squeezed the bejesus out of them...

...which seemed to drive him on all the more...and which caused Mike Matthews great joy. And he stroked his cock harder and HARDER, determined to cum till it was good to the last drop...

Finally, though, when Archie couldn't cum anymore, he, with his teeth clenched and sopped in sweat, slowly slid his spent manhood from Mike Matthews' hole...

"AWWWWWWWW GOD," Archie whined. "Like you would say, Mr. Matthews, what a day this turned out to be..." he said while panting.

Archie flopped down on the bed next to the well-muscled finance executive. Mr. Matthews let go of his spent cock, gathered the redheaded college freshman into his manly arms, kissed his cheek, and said, "Your cock feeling drained there, Carrot Top?"

Loving the feel of the older man's arms around him, Archie smiled and said, "Yeah, sort of, Mr. Matthews, but I'm sure that later on, after some rest and some food, I'll be ready and raring to go again. As I said, I plan to spend more than just the morning with you here today...unless you really need me to leave so you can get to your Wall Street work..."

Using his brute strength, Mike Matthews grabbed Archie by his upper arms, hoisted him up a bit, and then held the college freshman tight so that his head was positioned directly over his massive chest...or, to be more precise, so Archie's head was positioned directly over his cum soaked chest...and pecs...and nipples...and stomach region...

With a smile on his face from ear to ear, the red-haired kid didn't need to be told what to do.

He pressed his palms against the bed, leaned his head down, and slowly began licking his cum from Mr. Matthews' chest, kissing the man's colossal pecs at the same time.

The sounds of Archie sucking his cum off the finance executive's chest filled the room.

"NICE Carrot Top, that feels real nice," Mike Matthews croaked, again running his fingers of both hands through Archie's hair. *"Carrot Top..."*

When the college freshman began sucking his cum off the finance executive's jutted-up nipples, Mr. Matthews reacted with a loud sounding, "AWWWWWW SHIIITTT Carrot Top, my nipples, my MAN TITS are still all sensitive feeling there...MAN TITS they are!"

The man gripped the bedsheets with his chest area arched up off the bed now. Archie grinned up at him and said, "Don't you know, Mr. Matthews, that after a man shoots a load, every part of him is super sensitive to the touch...and suck...just like your nips are at this moment...

Before the finance executive could reply, Archie leaned his head back down and slurped the man's other cum coated nipple into his mouth...

...and sucked hard...

"HUHHHHHH you weren't just blowing air there, kid, fucking Carrot Top, my nipples, my MAN TITS feel like they're alive on my goddamned chest, yeah, that's it you lunatic kid, suck my sensitive nipples, eat my cum off them, hearty and good for you..." Mike Matthews' voice was demanding, and his tone bossy. He again ran his fingers through Archie's flaming red hair.

A few minutes later, when all of the man's cum had been sucked off his nipples, Mike Matthews was once again roaring and grunting in disbelief. Archie had hoisted his legs upward and slid his newly erect cock inside him yet again...

"HUHHHHHH, FUCKING FUCKS Carrot Top, you're a goddamned twenty-four-hour erection! GAWWWD, *cock up my ass*, you lunatic kid, fucking cock up my ass!" the finance executive couldn't hold it anymore, and he blubbered joyfully...

/The End/

(Near?) Humiliating Experience

Inspired by: Timmy Backman

I WAS BABYSITTING MY BROTHER'S DOG, and while out walking him on a warm and sunny Saturday afternoon, I stopped to chat with a neighbor couple. They were in their backyard and came up to the waist-high fence when they saw me wave hello. I thought it would be nice to say hello back, so I stopped to chat a bit. The gate to the backyard was open. Upon seeing the dog I had on the leash, my neighbor's two-year-old grandson came bounding out of the yard. His eyes were wide, and he kept smiling as he approached my brother's dog, a two-year-old Jack Russell named Rex.

Rex was instantly smitten with the two-year-old Tyler. His tail was wagging at what looked to be hundreds of miles an hour as the young boy petted him and cooed, "Nice doggy, nice doggy," at him.

"Looks like Tyler likes this dog, Timmy," my neighbor, a hulking guy named Jack, who was in his mid to late fifties, said to me as he sidled up at the fence where I was standing.

"Yeah! He belongs to my brother Bruce and his partner. They got him a few months ago. His name is Rex," I said, standing there dressed for the warm weather in a pull-over teal colored short-sleeved polo shirt, khaki shorts that came down to my thighs, black calf-length dorky-looking nylon dress socks, and brown lace-up Dockers. "I'm taking care of him while Bruce and his partner are away on a two-week vacation. They asked me and Stephanie if we would mind babysitting Rex here."

"Rex!" two-year-old Tyler exclaimed as he continued petting the dog.

As Jack smiled down at his grandson petting the dog, Jack's wife, a very still pretty woman in her early fifties named Margie, sauntered over to us. She stood next to her built-like-a-brick shithouse husband. I had to wonder just how often Jack worked out, seeing as his biceps and triceps were the size of boulders and bulging from the short sleeves of the white tee shirt he had on.

"Hi Timmy, how are you today?" Margie asked me, looking almost hungry. I thought she smiled at me, but I quickly pushed the thought away.

"Doing well, thanks, Margie," I replied. "My word, but Tyler is growing up so fast. I can't believe he's already two years old."

At the sound of me saying his name, Tyler turned his attention to me. He smiled up at me and waved.

"Can you say hi to Mr. Backman Tyler?" Jack asked his grandson.

"Hi, Mr. Backnan," the little boy said, mispronouncing my name just a bit, causing us adults to giggle good-naturedly.

"So, where did your brother and his partner go on their vacation?" Jack asked me.

I wanted to tell Jack that I could not have given a rat's ass where my brother and his partner had gone on their vacation. After Bruce's latest tickle trick that he had managed to get over on me, I REALLY, REALLY could not have cared less where he was...but I didn't say that to Jack and Margie.

Instead, I said, "They're spending two weeks in Europe."

"Nice, very nice! Lucky you and Stephanie that you get to spend two weeks with that adorable and oh so cute dog," Margie said.

"Yes, indeed we do," I said, trying not to sound too sarcastic, seeing as when Bruce had asked me and Stephanie to babysit Rex for two weeks, I was set to answer him with a seething "NO," but it was Stephanie who agreed that we would mind the dog, God love her.

As my two neighbors and I were chatting, Tyler stopped petting Rex. He came over to me and squatted down at my feet. He was a cute little tyke, and I smiled down at him.

"Mr. Backnan back cocks," Tyler giggled, and I nearly gasped when he closed his tiny hands around one of my black-socked calves.

Oh my, those little fingers...Oh! If he had been 30 years older, I would have known exactly what he was doing. But, since he was just two, it was totally innocent. But, the effect on me was the same tingling little stimulants running up my legs.

"Oh my, isn't that cute?" Margie exclaimed, grinning. "Tyler seems to like your black socks, Timmy, even though he called them back cocks, hee, hee, hee..."

"Uh, yes, yes, he did at that," I said, all of us adults now glancing down and watching as little Tyler pushed my black sock down a tad and then took it by the top section and pulled it back up.

Tyler's eager little fingers and the mere mention of the word cock made my balls rumble.

"Well, I'll be," Jack said and ruffled my hair a bit as Tyler again tugged my sock down and pulled it back up. "Looks like my grandson found himself a new toy, eh Timmy?"

Oh my god...I'm a toy! Oh, I've been a toy before, I thought as my balls rumbled some more.

"Yeah, I would suppose he did at that," I giggled, sounding stupid and nervous at the same time.

What was adding to this situation and my dilemma was the fact that ever since Master Doug decreed it, I have been going commando...*no underpants.*

Master Doug was the guy I had relinquished control of my cock to...a virtual Master, but a Master just the same. He said how not wearing underpants would make me always mindful of my cock, which it absolutely did...AND does. So, while my cock was not hard and excited when I approached my neighbors, it was now awake and ready for action.

"So Timmy, how is Stephanie doing?" Margie asked me. "I haven't seen her lately."

Margie's question served to pull my attention partially away from the teasing action happening on my bare legs.

"She uh, she's fine Margie," I responded, feeling like I was sweating a bit now as Tyler had gone to work playing with my other sock, pulling it down to my ankle area and then stretching it back up again, oh my word how visions of that so-called buddy of mine, Ronald, danced in my tortured mind. "Stephanie has been helping her friend Valerie Levi out with her import-export business, so she's been really busy with that and such. I would suppose that's why you haven't seen her lately. I will tell her you were asking."

Meanwhile, the little hands that were groping my legs and playing with my socks were sending chills up my legs, rattling my asshole, and continuing up my spine, making the hair on the back of my neck stand up. In addition, my cock, leaped at the stimulation causing an immediate bulge in my shorts. And my balls tightened and rolled in their sac.

"Ah, I know Valerie," Jack mused as he sauntered out of the gate now and stood beside me and his grandson, who seemed to have become hypnotized by playing with my danged black socks, of all things, switching off from my left to my right as he tugged them down and then up again.

Even my tormentor, Ronald, could not have devised a tortuous stimulation any better than those little hands and fingers exploring my legs and socks.

At one point, Tyler left my right sock down near my ankle as he played with the left one, and then when the left one was pulled down to my ankle, he pulled the right one up to my calf again. Yep! That little boy had really made a plaything out of my socks and had managed to click on my sexual switch as well. Oh, my word, again! I was now worried that my condition would be noticeable.

"You uh, you know Valerie?" I asked Jack, tugging on my shirt collar, seeing as I wasn't wearing a tie to tug on at that moment, my nervous tic.

And seeing as Jack had just said that he knew Valerie and seeing as my danged trademark tickle socks were being played with in a whole new fashion of sorts, well, I would say that I, ticklish Timmy Backman, had LOTS to be nervous about at that moment. Jack mentioning Valerie's name made the tickle memories flood into my brain, and his grandson was setting fire to my legs. Oh my! But the heat in my shorts was reaching a boiling point.

"Sure as heck I know Valerie," Jack said, grinning from ear to ear now as he coiled a huge hand around one of my upper arms and held it tight. "That is one really amazing woman."

"UM, amazing?" I asked as Jack squeezed my arm, and Margie was most definitely looking at me hungrily.

And I could have sworn that she stole a look at my crotch, which didn't help my confidence at that point. I could feel sweat begin to pop out on my forehead.

"Well, yeah! Owning her own business and all..." Jack said and squeezed my arm tighter.

As Jack and I spoke and Margie drank me in with her eyes, AND Tyler played with my danged socks, my brother's stupid dog simply wagged his tail, looking around, obviously wondering when we were going to continue our walk.

"Oh yes, that, yes, that does make Valerie an amazing woman, I suppose," I said, turning my head and grinning at Jack as he held my arm in an almost loving embrace now.

But then, the next instant, everything went to hell... Why? Because Tyler decided to abandon my danged socks, leaving them both pulled only halfway up, making them look ridiculous and decided then that he was going to play with my khaki shorts.

I stood there holding the dog's leash in hand, trying to make conversation with my neighbors, Jack and Margie. Meanwhile, little Tyler stood up, reached to the top...and grabbed the sides of my shorts. Now, he began tugging on them. Damn! My sexual buttons had already been pushed. But, the sudden tug on my shorts caused a whole new wave of humiliating embarrassment to flood my brain and make my cock leap in my shorts. Flashing through my mind's eye was the visual of little Tyler tugging my shorts down, leaving me bare ass naked below the waist.

"Now, Tyler, playing with Mr. Backman's socks was one thing, but playing with his shorts now? Mr. Backman wouldn't appreciate you pulling his shorts down." Margie said with a smile and a lustful look in my direction.

She did not sound disciplinary at all as she admonished Tyler for what he was suddenly doing.

"Tyler! Don't be pulling on Mr. Backman's shorts...you just might pull them down." Margie said again...but there was total hunger in her eyes, as if she was willing it to happen what she was admonishing Tyler for.

"Oh, uh, oh my word," I muttered, glancing down at the little boy as he had literally hung himself on my shorts, seeing as his little sneakered feet were a few scant inches off the ground, giving him all the more leverage on my shorts.

Now, because of my Internet Master, Master Doug, I was no longer permitted to wear underpants. He had taken control of me and my penis via the internet. He had commanded that until he decreed otherwise, I was to go commando in my suit pants, casual pants, and yes, even in my walking shorts.

Master Doug was also the reason I was wearing dorky black nylon dress socks with my Dockers that day. Seeing as my Internet Master wanted me always reminded of my ticklish trials...and how I was always in my black socks, it seemed for those danged trials of mine.

"Oh my goodness, isn't that just so cute though?" Margie exclaimed stupidly as her darling grandson hung himself up even tighter on my shorts, pulling them downward as he did so, and after she had told him NOT to play with my danged shorts, oh my word, oh my fucking word. "First, Tyler was playing with your black socks. Now he's playing with your shorts, Timmy. It looks to me like my grandson has really taken a shine to you."

The lustful look in Margie's eyes told me she was enjoying my predicament, and she was really not doing anything to come to my assistance.

"Yeah, so he is, and so he has," I said, standing there sweating in my danged, pulled-halfway-down black socks that Margie had just mentioned. "But if it's all the same to you, Margie, I would rather the little guy play with my socks rather than my shorts...and..."

Just when I was speaking, little Tyler landed on his feet, still holding onto the sides of my shorts...and lo and fucking behold, ripped and downward went my shorts.

"OH MY, *oh my word!*" I bantered madly, SO, SO very aware of the fact at that moment that I was totally naked under my shorts and that I was now totally exposed to the world.

"Oh no, Tyler, *Tyler,* you bad boy, now look what you did to Mr. Backman's shorts. You ripped them on both sides," Margie scolded her two-year-old grandson. "You bad boy, and after I told you to play with his socks and not his shorts. Oh, you bad boy, you get in the house right this instant, now!"

Margie said the words, but she licked her lips and seemed to relish my now-exposed erection.

Tyler simply giggled, yelled out, "Mr. Backnan's shorts!" and scampered into the house. I didn't see the little brat for the rest of the day, but I sure, as all fucks and tarnation, did see Jack and Margie.

"I'm so sorry, buddy," Jack said to me from where he was still standing at my side, still gripping my arm tight and just looking at my bobbing cock below my shirt.

I stood there stupidly with my ripped shorts bunched at my ankles and my flaming erection standing straight out and unable to do anything. I had Rex's leash in one hand, and Jack had me by the other arm. I was helplessly exposed.

"Oh my, here, Timmy, I'll take Rex and leash him in the yard," Margie said, coming out of the gate, taking Rex's leash from me and licking her lips as she eyed my bobbing member. "Jack, get poor Timmy in the house so I can mend his shorts."

"What? Oh, yeah, okay, yeah, leash Rex, mend my shorts, I guess," I stammered, not really aware of the fact that Margie had taken Rex's leash from me and was bringing the dog into the yard, the dog that if I hadn't had to walk, I would not be losing my shorts at that moment.

I was still fixated on trying to pull up and secure a pair of shorts that, no matter what I did, WOULD not stay up anymore. How in all fucks was I going to get into Jack and Margie's house so that no one around would see my ruined shorts...AND possibly see my condition of commando and my flaming erection at that?

"My gosh, Timmy, I'm so sorry," Jack exclaimed from next to me, STILL holding my arm tight, nearly possessively at that point it seemed, and it was not lost on me that he had definitely noticed I was commando with a major erection under my ruined shorts. "I don't know what all got into Tyler..."

"Yeah, me either," I snorted irritably, STILL trying at the same time to pull my shorts up as they kept falling.

"C'mon buddy, let's do what Margie said and get you into the house so she can mend those shorts of yours, huh?" Jack asked, and in a FAST, sweeping motion, the stack of muscles wrapped one huge arm around my upper body, his other arm under my legs, and hoisted me up off the ground and into his gargantuan arms in the position of a groom carrying his bride over the threshold on their wedding night. "And I'll make sure no one sees that you got no under drawers on, HEH!"

"Uh yeah, what uh.... Whatever. Thanks for the lift, I suppose I should say, Jack," I muttered, throwing one arm around the guy's shoulders as he carried me toward the open door of the house.

"Margie will have those shorts of yours fixed in no time, buddy," Jack said, lugging me as if I were a featherweight...DANG... and was the big guy eyeing my erection as he lugged me?

As we neared the house, I crossed my calves in front of me, noting my danged, pushed-down black socks that had started this whole mess. Because a cute little boy named Tyler had taken a danged shine to push my socks down and up. And as Jack brought me into the house, I heard Rex barking happily. The dog seemed delighted in my latest plight.

Jack kicked the door closed behind him and lumbered with me toward a flight of stairs and down into the basement of the house...which I quickly saw was made up into a home gym with every conceivable weight machine one could imagine. My cock twitched harder, and I wrapped both arms around Jack's shoulders at that point.

/To Be Continued.../

(Near?) Humiliating Experience (Chapter Two)

AFTER JACK CARRIED ME DOWN THE STAIRS and to his home basement gym, he sat me down on a stool. As he did, I untwined my arms from around his huge bodybuilder-sized shoulders, somewhat reluctantly, I might add.

The way the guy had scooped me up and carried me into his house, rescuing me in a way from having my exposed erection seen by passersby, well, it all just felt so romantic and like something out of an old noir film where the hero rescues his sidekick. And let's face it, Jack carrying me into his house was a far cry from what Ronald had done the time he had snagged me for use in his infamous tickle palace AND carried me out of my house in the wee hours of the night. My God and my word, but how the memories of those days of my ticklish trials haunt me till now.

"Now, Timmy, let's get those ruined shorts off you so Margie can make some repairs," Jack stated and quickly pulled what was remaining of my khaki shorts off my legs, leaving me now in just my pull-over teal-colored polo shirt and black socks, jeez.

Holding my shorts up, the fucking muscle-headed guy was suddenly ogling at my naked lower half...and my large excited cock, which was sticking straight up out of my lap like a goddamned flagpole.

"Timmy, buddy, you seem to be very excited about these recent events. I can't imagine what happened to you making my cock hard, but yours is certainly agitated, it would seem. And what's with the no underpants? I think it's been proven today that not wearing underpants is a dangerous choice for you," Jack said, as he was leering at my nakedness... AND licking his lips.

My stripping at the hands of a two-year-old, the lustful look on Jack's face, my danged nakedness, and his questioning all combined to further embarrass me. It also caused further cock stimulation. My manhood stretched to the fullest and bounced in the cool basement air, dripping oodles of pre cum I might add.

"I...uh...well...it's just...I can...you see, Jack, there is definitely an explanation here, a strange explanation, but an explanation nonetheless..." I stuttered in my exposed and embarrassed state. "You see, I got myself involved in a masturbation addiction website, and I met a guy online that I thought was going to help me. Instead, I wound up relinquishing control of my penis and my orgasms to him...and I'm unable to break free of his control. You see, this guy ordered me, Doug is his name, but I call him Master Doug, to never, NEVER wear underpants."

"Very interesting, very interesting indeed, a masturbation addiction website," Jack said, scratching his chin. "And judging from that skyscraper you're sporting between your legs there, buddy, I would surmise that it's been a while since this Master Doug permitted you even one orgasm."

"It's been months, Jack, months, and I'm so horny. I can't believe it," I admitted. "And my balls ache like nothing I've ever known. Talk about a case of runaway blue balls, eh?" I said sounding despondent yet at the same time, so very proud of myself.

"So you're saying that no matter what happens, NO MATTER WHAT, you aren't permitted at this time to have an orgasm?" Jack asked me, sounding devious as all hell as he spoke.

I simply nodded my response, not even wanting to say the words and admit that he was right, that at this time, I was not permitted to have an orgasm.

About that same time, Margie came down the basement steps.

"Well, Rex is playing in the yard, and little Tyler just zonked out for his nap. Now, where are Timmy's shorts...oh my, oh my, my, what a beautiful cock you have, Timmy!" Margie bellowed in shock and confidently stepped forward for a better view of my raging erection, my raging erection that I had done nothing to conceal as she had come down the steps to the basement.

Margie moved closer and closer to me, seeming like she was hypnotized, until she suddenly reached out and grasped my throbbing frustrated cock with one hand. Awww, GAWD, and then she proceeded to stroke my highly sensitive sex muscle.

I groaned loudly, trying to tell Margie not to make me cum, that I was not allowed at that time to cum, but suddenly, my thoughts were cut off. Margie let go of my erection when I heard Jack roar, "HEY, what in all hell is going on now? Are you trying to seduce my wife? Well, we'll just see about that!"

And with that, Jack reached down, grabbed me by my black socked ankles, and hoisted me up yet again, this time in an upside-down position, with my head dangling over the floor.

"YULLLLPPP! Hey, Jack, be careful here, bud!" I barked, my arms flailing uselessly at my sides as Jack lugged me toward a metal chin-up bar that was set up in a concrete archway. "No, man, I'm not trying to seduce your wife...she..." I was stopped midway.

But as I was about to try to tell Jack that it was actually Margie who had been trying to seduce me, Margie herself yanked my Dockers off my feet...and quickly replaced them with padded metal rings, inversion boots actually, boots without any boots. Then, Jack hoisted me up higher and literally hung me up on the chin-up bar, upside down, using the inversion boots to secure me to the bar.

"AWWWWWWHHHH!" I moaned miserably, arching my head forward and looking up from the blasted position I now found myself in, woe is me. Oh, my word again! Jack then held my arms behind me, and Margie quickly lashed my wrists tightly together with Velcro bindings. "JACK, MARGIE, please...PLEASE... lemme down! What's the point of this?"

"The point, Timmy, my good neighbor?" Jack laughed, stepped behind me, grabbed my thighs, and spread my legs apart as I hung there. "The point is to show you that one should NOT sneak up on their neighbors while one is not wearing proper under dressings."

As Jack spread my legs, my cock stuck out harder than steel, pointing at Margie, as she stood there, taking in my predicament, or more precisely, in the words of Tickle Master Vince, my pre-DICK-a-ment. Margie was smiling gleefully, as that bitch that she had turned out to be!

"Oh my God! But Jack? Dude, I explained all that to you and..." I began to clarify myself, but it was too late...oh my word of words then...UHHH, my eyes crossed in my head, my balls seemed to shift in their sac, and my cock dripped more pre cum as Jack grabbed my ass cheeks, spread them wide apart, and spit a few times into my asshole. "UHHH..."

The fucking guy was then massaging my hole with two, then three fingers, really prodding his digits inside me.

FUCK, but it felt like the guy was digging for gold in my stink hole... JEEEEZZZZ!

Margie watched, seemingly transfixed, as her husband teased my hole and how it was indeed causing my hard cock to twitch in the wind.

"OH LORD, Jack, Jack, *what in all hell...*" I panted from my position of utter helplessness.

Once more, my words were cut short as Jack positioned himself closer to me, held my ass cheeks wider apart, and plunged his tongue into my exposed, wet, and gaping asshole.

"AWWWWWWWHHHHHHHHHH! OH MY, oh my, what, what all are you up to up there, Jack?" I railed through clenched teeth, my toes curling back under my danged trademark black tickle socks. The fucking guy then dribbled liberally into my anal canal and sucked it up real heartily; making loud slurping noises as he did so. "M-Margie, Margie, please, please talk some sense into your husband...because what he's doing does not make sense! AWWWWWW MEEEEEEEE!" I screamed.

"Oh, Timmy! Obviously, you don't really know that husband of mine," Margie said, sounding dumber than a dumb blonde. "Once Jack sets his mind to something, there is no stopping him at all." She marveled at her husband's annoying obstinacy.

"So I've gathered," I blubbered crazily.

Then, from my upside-down position, I watched as Margie stepped over to me, ran her palms up and down over the fronts of my thighs, and breathlessly said to her husband, "Oh Jack, he looks so sexy here the way you hung him up," and proceeded to press her mouth against my dangling ball sac, licking it hungrily as she did so.

I let out a screeching sound that was almost womanly as I was now being feasted on from two ends. My balls were boiling now, and my cock was stretched to the limit. Pre cum was literally pouring from my piss slit and dripping all over the front of Margie's blouse.

"OOOOOOOOOOOOOOOOOO...OOOOOOO..." Jack, Margie, I-I can't...I'm not permitted to cum," I panted madly. "And with what you're both doing to me here, I'm liable to do just that...*cum...*"

I was gasping and gurgling crazily, wanting to cum so bad, really, but wanting more than anything to adhere to Master Doug's rules. And I knew that if I shot my load, I would have to report it to Master Doug.

"AHHHH, no worries, Timmy," Jack said, raising his face from out of my hole for a moment so he could speak." Me and Margie won't touch that erection of yours...we'll just have our romp and then send you home, hornier than you were though when you first got here...But there is one thing I want from you. I want your Master Doug's email address. I think Margie and I can be part of this equation."

That said, Jack plunged his mangy tongue back into my hole and resumed slurping and sucking on it...as his wife teased my testicles with her mouth and tongue...

Oh, my word, but my neighbors were making me loonier than a loon. Of course, I knew that even if I did not cum that day, I WOULD have to report this to Master Doug... And, oh god, if Master Doug turned them loose on me, I would no longer be safe in my own neighborhood.

A short while later, Jack and Margie had stripped down to nakedness... Jack took me down from the chin-up bar, left my hands bound behind me, set me atop a massage-style table on my back, lifted my legs into the air, grabbed my socked calves, yanked me forward to the end of the table, spread my legs apart, exposing my hole once more, and this time plunged his huge thickly veined erection into it...as his just as horny wife straddled my face at the other end, her pussy over my mouth. Without having had to tell me what to do, I licked Margie's pussy...as her husband fucked my stink hole.

As my hole was fucked and as I serviced Margie's pussy I thought how my neighbors would be granted sexual release this afternoon...and I, of course, would not. **OH MY GOD**, but how the sounds of an ass being fucked and a pussy being licked filled the room as the bottoms of my socked feet stared up at the ceiling...

Epilogue...

An hour and a half later, I was walking home with Rex on his leash. My shorts had been mended. When I left Jack and Margie's house, my asshole was feeling really stretched and used and fucked, and drunk seeing as after he had shot his load inside me, he claimed it back again, drinking his cum from my hole. While Margie had three violent orgasms in a row as I ate her pussy, and twisted my nipples to spur me on all the more...

When I got home, I set Rex free from his leash so he could bound around the house.

And as for me, I sat down in front of my computer to email my afternoon exploits to Master Doug, glad that I did not have to report having cum, though...LOL...and with Jack and Margie having Master Doug's email address, I wondered how my home life would change.

/The End/

Mr. Thomas Vischel's Socks and Feet

IT WAS FRIDAY NIGHT. At 5:15 pm, I was ready for the weekend and a three-day weekend at that...

I had planned to join some of my buddies for a few beers after work at our usual watering hole in the Wall Street area in New York City where we all worked, all of us, meaning us Wall Street bulls...

But on that particular Friday night, of all Friday nights, I was running late in getting my last-minute debit cards, company checks, and requisition papers signed off on by Mr. Thomas Vischel, the man who behind his back most of us called TV, the VP of the department I work for at the reputable brokerage house.

My name is Barry Richardson. I'm 22 years old, and working for the prestigious brokerage firm was my first job out of college...

...and all I wanted during my first few months there was to impress Mr. Thomas Vischel with my intense work ethic and with how I always managed to get things done on time...or to get things done *before* they were due.

But on that Friday, and before a three-day weekend at that, it seemed as if the cards had been stacked in my disfavor. Because of endless phone calls from clients, a damned computer glitch, and a text-wise argument with my girlfriend, Sara, I was, for the first time in my few months at the firm, behind in my work.

It wouldn't have been so bad if it was just the office supervisor that I needed to have to sign off on my work documents. No, it had to be the top VP of the company, Thomas Vischel, Mr. TV himself...

So at 5:15 pm and with a folder full of documents in hand, I was dashing down the hall from my work area toward Mr. Vischel's private office and praying he was still there and hadn't left early to get his three-day weekend started...

As I was dashing faster down the hall, I saw Mr. Vischel's private secretary, Janice, just shutting off her computer at the reception desk directly in front of the man's private office, his domain as it was called.

"Good evening, Janice," I said, practically out of breath as I stopped in my tracks at her reception desk.

She took in the sight of me with my tie pulled down a bit, my top shirt button undone, and the look of stress on my blond-haired, blue-eyed face.

Fuck! As she looked at me, I realized I had forgotten to put on my suit jacket. It was a rule that whenever ANYONE, anyone, especially a new employee such as me, wanted an audience with Mr. Vischel, you had to be completely, corporately attired...and that meant that where men in the company were concerned, we had to be fully suited...DAMN!

"Good evening, Barry," Janice replied. "Is something the matter?"

Holding up my folder of documents that required Mr. Vischel's signature and gesturing at the closed door of the man's office, I asked, "Is Mr. Vischel still here? I need to get his signature on these documents before I leave for the night."

Janice nodded and said, "Yes, he's still here."

"Oh, thank God," I exclaimed.

Janice picked up her desk phone, placed the receiver to her ear, pressed a button on the phone console, and said, "Barry Richardson is here, Mr. Vischel. He needs you to sign off on some documents."

Janice paused for a moment, then said, "Yes, Sir," and hung up the phone. "You can get right in," she said.

I thanked Janice and wished her a happy three-day weekend as she headed toward the elevators. I walked into Mr. Thomas Vischel's office, closing the door behind me.

I expected to find the man seated behind his gargantuan desk, but instead, he was in a leather chair with his feet propped up on a hassock that matched the chair he was seated in...

"Good evening, Mr. Vischel," I said as I stood a few feet away from the VP...

...and took in the fact that he had his lace-up wingtip shoes off, his thin black socked feet propped up on the hassock in front of him...

...and for some damned unexplainable reason, I found myself unable to look away from those feet of his...

...those at least size 13, beefy, STRONG-looking feet, one crossed over the other...

...in his thin, silky, very expensive-looking black dress socks...

"Good evening to you, Mr. Richardson," the rugged-looking, dark-eyed, dark-haired, and bearded VP replied, causing my attention to be pulled away from those big black socked feet of his...

...for the moment...

"Everything okay there, Barry?" he asked me, looking up from the stack of papers he was holding.

"Uh, yes, yes, Sir. I uh, just need for you to sign off on these documents, and I'll be out of your way," I said.

"Do you think you're in my way, Barry?" the VP asked me, setting aside the stack of papers he had been holding...and wiggling his toes under his socks...

"I, uh, well..." I replied.

"Barry, relax, have a seat," Mr. Vischel said with a grin, indicating a chair...which just happened to be set up directly next to the hassock that his socked feet were propped up on. "And let me have a look at those documents you need me to sign off on..."

"Yes, Sir, sure thing," I said, sitting down in the chair, staring downward...at those damned HUGE silk-socked feet of the VP...

...and again he was wiggling his toes under those silk socks...those black silk socks that I could suddenly smell now, a slight but pungent odor of leather, male feet sweat, and DEFINITE masculinity emanating from them...

"Barry...Barry..." Mr. Vischel was calling out to me, but somehow, it wasn't registering...

... as I was too transfixed by his huge silk-socked tootsies...And the way he was wiggling his toes under those socks was, for whatever the fuck reason driving me totally batty...

"Earth to Barry, earth to Barry..." Mr. Vischel called to me again, and this time, it did register. My head popped up, and I looked at him.

"Something the matter, Barry?" the VP asked me, setting aside my stack of documents and placing them on top of the papers he had been looking at when I had entered his office.

"Uh, no, Sir," I replied nervously, and to my utter shock, the man hefted his socked feet up a bit and off the hassock.

"Probably it's my socks. I know how they can smell at the end of the day," Mr. Vischel said. The sound of those words caught my breath in my throat. "But I really like to relax this way at the end of the day with my shoes off, and since it was the end of the day, I didn't expect to have anyone in here in my office...to smell my socks..."

"No, Sir. I would suppose not. I know you didn't expect to have someone here at the end of the day...to smell your socks," I said and took a deep breath, realizing what he meant about the smell coming from his socked feet...

...and now that he had hefted those socked feet up a bit, I realized the smell was even more pungent than I had originally thought...and the smell of the sweaty silk mixed with leather mixed with male foot sweat was even more intoxicating somehow...

"You know Barry, it's funny," Mr. Vischel said, wiggling his toes even more now under his socks, AND hefting his feet up even higher, within my reach...OMG...

"It's uh, it's funny, Sir?" I asked him.

"Yeah, when I get home from work, my wife insists that I put my socks right into the washing machine after I take them off. She doesn't even want them in the laundry basket. She says they smell so bad that she doesn't even want to handle them to put them in the washing machine. She even told me that our maid said the same thing..." Mr. Vischel said, looking at me intently as he spoke...

"Your wife and your maid are fools," I said softly, not believing the words that had just fallen out of my mouth.

"I'm sorry, Barry," Mr. Vischel said and lowered his socked feet back down onto the hassock. "What was that you just said about my wife and maid?"

In response, instead of answering the VP verbally, I leaned forward in my seat, reached down, and boldly grabbed Mr. Vischel's socked feet in a firm grip...and hoisted them upwards...

"What in the..." the VP exclaimed, gripping the arms of his chair now.

"I said your wife and maid are fools, Mr. Vischel," and as I said it, suddenly feeling totally emboldened for whatever the fucking reason, I moved my face close to the man's socked feet in my hands, gripping them tighter now by his muscular calves and ankles.

I pressed my nose and mouth against the little toe of Mr. Vischel's right foot and sniffed...and deeply inhaled the musty manly odor...

"Your socked feet smell great, Mr. Vischel," I said breathlessly and sniffed and inhaled the glorious funky odor again...this time even planting a few very wet-lipped kisses on the side of the man's right foot...

...and lo and fucking behold, his toes were now wiggling under his socks at what appeared to be hundreds of miles per hour...

"J-Jesus, what in all hell are you doing, Barry?" the VP exclaimed as I held his hoisted socked feet tighter yet and pressed my nose and mouth harder against them...sniffing and kissing them...*sniffing and kissing them*... "Y-you're sniffing and kissing my damned feet here, Barry!"

In response, I also began squeezing and kneading the man's socked feet...

"AH fuck, massaging them too..." Mr. Vischel panted then...

Holding his feet tight in my two-handed grasp, I left the chair I was sitting in and positioned myself on the floor, on my knees...directly in front of the VP's silk-socked tootsies...

With no hesitation whatsoever, I stuck out my tongue and began licking the bottoms of the man's socked feet alternately, REALLY pressing my tongue against the beefy flesh under those thin black silk socks of his...licking them the same way I would lick ice cream from a cone...

"AWWW fuck, fucking fucks," the VP rasped in a husky-sounding tone of voice. "I hate to admit it, Barry, but that feels fucking awesome...JEEZ, I can actually feel that in my cock, the way you're licking my damned smelly socks...HA! What a thing, licking my smelly socks! My wife and maid would never believe it..."

As he spoke and as I continued doing what I was doing, my own cock was engorging in my suit pants...

Frankly, I could not believe what I was doing. I had never thought of another dude's socks as being sexy or erotic...but there I was, on my knees, holding my VP's socked tootsies in my hands and sniffing and lapping at his socks as if they were the best tasting and smelling things on God's green Earth...

"MY wife wouldn't believe it...FUCK, *I don't believe it...*" the VP went on, him now watching intently as I licked, licked, and LICKED the bottoms of his silk-socked feet.

I should add here just how hot the silk of Mr. Vischel's socks felt against my tongue as I did my work...

Then, I spread the man's big feet apart and slowly, so slowly slithered my tongue up and down his deep and sexy arches...

"AWWWW, now that feels amazing, Barry...FUCKING amazing..." the VP moaned, now really gripping the arms of his chair as he watched me.

And I saw the HUGE bulge he was sporting in the crotch section of his suit pants...

I held the VP's big feet tight by the balls of them and lowered my head even further down between them, really pressing the tip of my tongue alternately against his arches and slithering it up and down, up and down, and sniffing at the same time...

"AWWWWWWW JEEEEEZ, I think I may make this part of your daily work description, Barry," Mr. Vischel chuckled. "Never before has anyone paid my socked feet such attention..."

Holding his socked feet tighter yet, I lifted my head up, looked Mr. Vischel straight in the eyes, and said, "I would be more than happy to have this as part of my daily work description, Mr. Vischel...and anyone who never paid attention to your socked feet before were idiots..."

With that, I raised my head over the tops of the VP's socked feet and closed my wet lips around his big toe and the first two other toes on his right foot and began sucking, HARD...

"AWWWW yeah, look at you there now, Barry, sucking my toes like they were my cock, FUCK, go ahead, suck all my sweaty juice out of those socks, Barry," Mr. Vischel said, panting like crazy. "Tonight when I get home, my socks won't stink...and my wife and my maid will be very surprised, I'm sure..."

I bobbed my head up and down on his toes, sucking them as if they were little cocks... although I've never sucked a cock before...

I moved my head over a bit and went to work sucking the last two toes of the VP's right foot, sucking them just as hard as I did the first three...and this time swirling my tongue round and round them at the same time...

"UHHHHHH, FFFUUUUCCCKK..." Mr. Vischel grunted, gripped the arms of his chair tighter yet, arched his head back, and jutted his crotch upwards... "Never thought I could get so aroused by someone working my feet...*and a dude at that*...go figure..."

"Yeah, go figure," I laughed and quickly resumed sucking the man's toes...

Then, holding his feet tight in my grip, I planted kisses over the toes of his right foot, my mouth tasting of the pungency that had been on his socks all over his toes.

"Get to work on my left toes now, Barry..." Mr. Vischel demanded then, lowering his head back and looking at me with eyes filled with outright lust.

"Yes, Sir," I replied and quickly and EAGERLY did as I was told...

After I had sucked all the sweaty juice out of the toes of Mr. Vischel's left foot's socked-toes, I went back again to licking and lapping at the bottoms of his socked feet...gripping his well-sucked toes as I did so, massaging them. God, his toes felt fantastic under those socks of his.

"Damn, Barry, I get the feeling we're going to be here a long while tonight before I sign off on those documents you brought to me," Mr. Vischel said, rubbing a hand over the bulge in the crotch section of his suit pants at that point...

I stopped licking the bottoms of Mr. Vischel's socked tootsies for a moment, looked up at him, and said, "Yes, Mr. Vischel, if you say so..." and resumed my task at hand...or, to be more precise, my task at feet...

/The End/

Thanking Their Coach

"**Awwwwwww Yeah,** yeah, fucking A, you guys, hoist me, hoist me, fucking rock me up and down on Lazarus's flagpole!" Soccer Coach Wilkins seethed at his two players at his sides, Manuel and Montello...as they did just as he had ordered them to. He took Lazarus's (his best player) cock deeper and deeper into his rear door with each hoist. "Great way to thank your coach for getting you guys to win the game!

And what a Fucking AWESOME way to celebrate winning the game today...AND against our arch-rival team at that, AWWWWWW YEAH, fill my hole with your pole, Lazarus!"

"Yeah, this is a great way to celebrate, Coach Wilkins," Manuel, dark-haired and goateed, exclaimed as he held his coach tight with the man's muscular arm draped over his ripped back and holding onto his broad shoulder for balance. "But I have to say I never heard of the legend you mentioned earlier...how if a team wins a game, the coach should be fucked and filled with his three best players' sperm...can't imagine how that hot girlfriend of yours feels about this..."

"YUHHHHHHHH...AWWWWW FUCCCCKKK YES," Coach Wilkins grunted as Lazarus's cock stretched his ass walls...as the handsome soccer player laid under him, and his two teammates did the chore of hoisting their beloved coach up and down and up and down on his erection. "It's no legend Manuel ol' boy...it's the God's honest truth... AWWWWWW YEAH, if a team wins a game and then the coach is fucked this way and filled with his three best players' manly juices, not their sperm, guys, their manly juices... sperm is for women, manly juices are for sport heads like us, soccer heads we are...so yeah, if the coach is fucked and filled with his three best players' manly juices it guarantees they'll win the next game...YUHHHHHHH, fucking fucks Lazarus, your cock feels like magic inside me, bud! And just for the record, Manuel, my hot girlfriend, Veronica, knows nothing about this. This is just between us soccer heads..."

"Feels pretty good down here as well, Coach Wilkins," Lazarus panted as he thrust, shoved, and plunged his erect cock deep inside his coach.

"So, with our manly juices sluicing inside you when we play our next game, how does that guarantee we'll win that next game, Coach?" Montello, bald and also goateed, asked the being skewered coach from the other side.

"It's simple, Montello. After a team wins a game and the three best players from that game fuck the coach and fill him with their manly juices, it brings luck, LUCK, luck for the coach and the entire team. AWWWWWWWW, Lazarus, I feel your cock churning in me...I think you're gonna spurt in me real soon! Rock me faster, you guys...*rock me faster!*"

As Manuel and Montello did as Coach Wilkins said, the muscles in their arms flexed crazily. They lifted and rocked their coach on their teammate's cock. The coach continued his tirade, "And just wait till we play our next game the day after tomorrow... AWWWWWW YEAH...your manly juices will have had enough time to work their way into my system that there's no way we'll lose that game against that other team that has been besting us lately...YUHHHHHHHHH...should have taken advantage of this old method of winning long ago!"

"But Coach, if what you're saying is true, isn't that cheating in a way?" Montello asked.

"Who gives a shit?" Lazarus grunted as he grabbed the coach's ass cheeks and fucked the man harder and harder. "Legend or not, fucking Coach Wilkins feels amazing. Just wait till it's your turn, buds...OH YEAH, rock the coach on my cock, you guys! Fuck! My girlfriend's pussy never felt this amazing!"

At that, all the men in the locker room laughed heartily...

Lazarus, then, breathlessly announced that he was about to cum, and Coach Wilkins grunted, "Go for it, bud. Fucking fill me with your manly juices! Cock my ass, Lazarus, fucking cock my ass! Dudes, jam me down on Lazarus's stalk! That way, his manly juices will really make their way inside me!"

The two young men did as their coach ordered, and with his head arched back, Coach Wilkins grunted like a captured marine as he felt Lazarus's manly juices filling him rear-wise...

"AWWWWW FUCK yes, fucking yes, that next team won't stand a chance against us the day after tomorrow. We're gonna cream them as bad as we creamed the so-called Vultures today!" Coach Wilkins bellowed.

"ARRRRHHHH, YEAH, gotta tell you guys, this is the most amazing experience I've ever had," Lazarus snarled under the coach, slapping the man's hard muscled ass cheeks as he seemed to endlessly cum and cum inside the man he had the utmost respect for.

"Stick with me, fellas, AWWWWWWW YEAH, and there'll be more and more of the same amazing experiences for you because if in the next game, three other players perform the best, they'll be fucking me!" the coach reeled.

"Then we better make sure we're the best players again at the next game," Montello stated as he held the coach tightly impaled on his teammate's sperming cock.

"ERRRRHHHHHH, good man Montello, good fucking man you are, and just for that positive comment, you get to fuck and fill me with your manly juices next!" Coach Wilkins exclaimed in jubilation.

When Lazarus's cock was spent, the three soccer players wasted no time in switching places, with Montello now sliding his erect cock in and out of the coach's cum soaked backdoor. Now, Manuel and Lazarus were hoisting their coach up and down.

"AWWWWWWW MAN, Montello, your cock feels as super in my hole as Lazarus's did, so fucking glad you three turned out to be the best players for today's game win, YUHHHHHHH, yeah that's it you soccer head, fuck your coach, fuck him and feed him your manly juices next!" Coach Wilkins swore and cussed, his own cock erect as a skyscraper, too...and oozing pre cum. "Cock my asshole Montello, fucking COCK THE STOCK out of my asshole!"

"Coach, does it always have to be three players that fuck the coach and fill him with their manly juices after the team wins a game?" Lazarus asked, his spent cock dribbling the last remnants of his ooze onto the locker room floor.

"YES, YES, AWWWWWW FUCKKKKK, yes," the coach replied.

"Why three?" Manuel asked as he and Lazarus hoisted their coach up and down on Montello's girth.

"Three is a magic number, guys. Remember the trinity, remember that three times is the charm, and look at how it's three of the best players of the moment cocking me in the ass," the coach explained. "AWWWWWW, fuck Montello, your cock is torturing my innards, you're touching my ass tonsils down there! Your cock is magic bud!"

"Your hole doesn't feel all that bad either, Coach," Montello huffed as he, like Lazarus before him, gripped Coach Wilkin's muscled ass cheeks and thrust his manhood deeper and deeper inside the man with each fuck. "FEELS amazing, man, and feels so good we can win the next game because of this..."

"We'll be winners for sure, my soccer heads," the coach grunted, and soon enough, he felt Montello's' warm, thick juices flooding him...as Lazarus and Manuel held him jammed down on the guy's spurting manhood. "AWWWWW YEAH, deep inside me, Montello, *deep inside me!*"

Once more, the three soccer players wasted no time...and then it was Manuel's turn to fuck the coach, as Lazarus and Montello hoisted the man up and down on his erect cock.

"AWWWWWWWW GODDDDDD, and on the third time, which - like I said - is the charm, I get to cum too with my three soccer heads," the coach blubbered, practically crying in joy and elation.

"FUCKING FUCKS, Coach, this is incredible!" Manuel reeled as he, like his two soccer buddies before him, slapped the coach's ass hard as he fucked him and fucked him.

"HUHHHHHHH, yeah, slap my ass cheeks Manuel; slap 'em hard, real fucking hard at that!" Coach Wilkins demanded. "It'll make me cum all the harder when I shoot my load...*my loads*...YUHHHHHHH!"

"Well, if you're gonna shoot your shot Coach Wilkins you'd better grab that flagpole between your legs and start strokin' and chokin'," Lazarus said, as he and Montello held their coach jammed down on the third cock that was fucking his ass that late afternoon in the locker room.

"NAH, naw, don't need to stroke and choke my meat stick, Lazarus ol' boy," Coach Wilkins gurgled as he felt Manuel's thick manly juices flooding his hole. "As I told you, soccer heads, number three is magic...and when the third mess of manly juices is filling me, I just cum...AWWWWWW...FUCK...I cum without my erection of steel having to be touched! And trust me, dudes, when a coach cums without his cock being touched, the feeling is electric! YUHHHHHH!"

And, true to his word, Montello and Lazarus watched in awe and amazement as their cock filled coach shot his load...his own mess of manly juices splattering all over his muscular chest and dripping sexily down onto his nipples, his stomach region, and into his thick patch of pubic hair.

"JEEZ Louise, if I didn't see it with my own damned eyes," Montello exclaimed as he and Lazarus continued holding their coach jammed down on Manuel's spurting cock, as it filled the man's hole...his hole being fed the third load of the afternoon.

Underneath the coach impaled on his erupting cock, Manuel grunted and gurgled, spanked the man's ass cheeks, and cummed like crazy inside him.

All the while, as Coach Wilkins himself spurted and squirted his mess, he went on and on ranting, "OH yeah, fucking A, third time is always the fucking charm...three IS the magic number..."

Finally, approximately ten minutes later, all four of the men were standing around the table where the three soccer players had all fucked their coach and filled him with their manly juices, their guarantee that they would win their next game.

"DAMN, can't thank you three soccer heads enough..." Coach Wilkins said. "Day after tomorrow, the proof will be in the pudding when we win the next game."

"More like the proof will be in the splooge," Lazarus said, and all four of the men laughed loudly, their booming voices echoing off the walls of the locker room.

"Sure as all hell, man," Coach Wilkins said and clapped Lazarus on the back. "Anyway, we better all get showered and dressed and get out of here..."

"Yep, sounds like a plan, Coach," Montello said.

As the three young men walked away from where the coach was standing, Manuel turned back and said, "Say, Coach, when we win the game the day after tomorrow, do we all get to fuck and fill you again with our manly juices?"

"Only if you're the three best players when we win, bud," the coach replied with a grin.

Manuel grinned back and said, "Looks like we'll be feedin' that ass of yours again real soon, Coach."

And as Manuel walked away toward the shower room at the other end of the locker room, the coach smiled from ear to ear.

"Guess I'd better get showered and be on my way as well," Wilkins mused softly. "YEAH, before the girlfriend starts to wonder what's takin' me so long in getting home."

Just then, from behind him, Coach Wilkins heard, "The girlfriend is going to have to wonder just a while more what's taking you so long to get home...*Coach Wilkins!*"

The coach whirled around on his socked feet, his spent cock flopping around as he did, and saw standing a few feet from him three soccer players from the rival team that his team had bested that day.

The coach knew all three of the soccer players' names: Brutus, Dudley, and Elmer.

As the three monstrously muscled young men sidled closer and closer to Wilkins, extracting their enormous erections from their uniform shorts, all the coach could whisper was, "Ah shit," because he knew all too well what the three rival team members had planned for him, because even though their team had lost the game, they had been the three best players that day.

A few moments later, Brutus was lying on the table on his back as Dudley and Elmer hoisted the overpowered Coach Wilkins up and down on his huge erection.

"Awwww, Gods, No!" Coach Wilkins thundered miserably. "Of all the fucked up twisted turns of events!"

"Got that right, Wilkins ol' boy," Dudley meanly razzed the newly being fucked soccer coach. "You see, we believe in that old legend as well, but in this case, we three believe in it in reverse...HA!"

As he was hoisted up and down on Brutus' mammoth-sized cock, Coach Wilkins seethed, "Yeah, if a coach is fucked and filled with the manly juices of three of the best rival team members, then that coach's team will fucking LOSE the next game...SHIT, shit, and more shit!"

"You got that right, Coach Wilkins..." Elmer laughed as he and Dudley rocked the man up and down on Brutus' soon-to-be spurting cock. "And all three of us are gonna fill you up nice and big!"

"Fucking bastards!" Wilkins ranted, saying to himself that he couldn't get his three best players to fuck and fill him again before their next game because the three times, the three fuck and fill superstition could only be done once before a next game.

And now, fucking fucks of all fucks, seeing that the three members of a rival team would be the last three to fuck and fill him before the next game, it meant that his team was now doomed to lose that next game. *DAMN, IT ALL!*

After Brutus shot his load inside the hapless coach, it wasn't long before Dudley took Brutus' place in fucking Coach Wilkins next, as Brutus and Elmer hoisted and rocked him up and down on the next cock filling his ass.

"RHHHHHHH!" Coach Wilkins roared, watching as his own cock had re-engorged between his legs. "FUCK, gonna cum again when Elmer gets his pole in my hole! *Damn it all to hell!*"

"Very Charlton Heston, I must say, Coach Wilkins," Elmer laughed as he and Brutus hoisted the coach up and slid him down on Dudley's erect cock. Repeating the action, squishing sounds filled the dank, musty-scented locker room air, as Dudley's meat speared the man's hole. "And when you shoot your load while I'm fucking you, your team will lose the game the day after tomorrow."

As the three rival team members laughed their heads off, Coach Wilkins leaned his head back. As Dudley's cock stimulated his anal opening, he wondered over how all would be lost the day after tomorrow.

A short while later...

Lazarus, Manuel, and Montello came out of the locker room shower area; all of them showered and dressed at that point. As they headed to the door to leave, they saw Coach Wilkins standing with his big hands pressed against the table, his head hanging down, and massive amounts of cum dripping from his asshole and down the backs of his muscular legs.

"Hey Coach, what are you still doing here?" Lazarus asked as he and his three teammates stepped over to their coach.

The coach turned around, his again spent cock swinging between his legs, a look of dejection on his face when he said, "Yeah guys, I'm still here, and I have some really bad news for all of you..."

/The End/

Hotel Housekeeping

I SUPPOSE IT CAN BE SAID IT was my own fault that it happened. And all because I had forgotten to change the doorknob sign on my hotel room door from "Please make up room" to "Do not disturb."

I was mentally exhausted from the three back-to-back meetings I'd had to attend that day in the hotel's conference room during the business trip I was on, so I suppose that was why I had forgotten to change the doorknob sign when I got back to my room that evening, after having had dinner in the hotel's dining room with my two work buddies.

When I had gotten to my private room in the top-of-the-line Diamond Hotel, I instantly stripped out of my suit and left it and my briefs on the bed. I padded on my socked feet to the bathroom, really wanting a nice hot tub of water to soak in before I went to sleep for the night. A nice hot soak in a tub always relaxes me.

It would relax me more if I could share that bath with my wife, but since I was on an out-of-town business trip, my wife was, of course, nowhere in attendance.

In the bathroom, I pulled the shower door open, put the drain stopper against the drain in the tub, and turned both the cold and hot water faucets to begin filling the tub.

I added some lavender-scented bath oil that the hotel supplied to the water, peeled my navy-blue nylon dress socks off my feet, hung them on an unoccupied spot of the towel rack, and sat down on the edge of the tub to wait till it was filled.

As I sat on the edge of the tub, I closed my eyes, and my cock did what I knew it would do. It grew hard and beefy, standing up long and straight between my well-toned and muscular legs.

For whatever reason, the scent of bath oils always gets my cock in full working order.

As I sat there with my eyes closed, listening to the sound of the running water as it filled the tub and breathing in the scent of the bath oil, I suddenly heard a woman's voice say, "Oh, oh my God...oh my..."

My eyes popped open, and I saw a hotel maid standing in the doorway of the bathroom.

"I-I'm sorry, Sir," the tall blond maid, appearing to be in her 30s, stammered as she stood there...her blue eyes stealing hungry-looking glances at my flagpole of an erection.

As my heart raced, my testicles seemed to shift in my sac, and pre-seed oozed from my cock slit and slid down my veiny shaft.

"I-I'm sorry, Mr. uh, Mr.," the very pretty maid stammered some more. "Mr. uh..."

"Robinson, John Robinson," I managed to croak.

"Mr. Robinson," the maid went on. "I'm so sorry, but the sign on your doorknob was turned to have the room made up."

"My, *my mistake*," I replied, but then, instead of backing off and out of the bathroom she was stepping slowly toward me. Me, who hadn't bothered to place my hands over my erection and low hangers.

Looking up at her, I saw that the nametag pinned to her black tight-fitting black uniform blouse read, "Teresa..."

And as she moved closer to me, I also saw that look of hunger on her face turn to one of absolute ravenousness.

A few seconds later, she was standing directly over me, looming over me. Actually, her black skirted crotch was staring me in the face.

"The bath water smells nice, Mr. Robinson," the maid said, sounding sexy as all hell.

"It's uh, it's lavender bath oil. I put it in there," I replied breathlessly.

She leaned over me, her good-sized cleavage under her uniform blouse brushing my face as she reached to turn off the water faucets of the now-filled tub.

"Don't want it to overflow, Mr. Robinson," she said, looking down at my erection.

I wondered if she was talking about the tub water overflowing or my cock.

My hands were shaking as my cock oozed more pre-seed. I ran my palms over the maid's shapely black silk stockinged thighs.

"T-Teresa..." I whispered dumbly as I looked up at her. "I-I'm a married man...*Teresa...*"

In response, she smiled down at me, squeezed my earlobes, and said, "So you are Mr. Robinson..." and with that, as I went on caressing her thighs, the feel of her silk stockings driving me crazy with lust, she stepped closer yet to me till her short-skirted crotch was pressed against my face.

She moaned contentedly as she went on playing with my earlobes.

I sniffed her crotch and stuck out my tongue, and my jaw dropped because what I felt my tongue pressing against was a throbbing erection under the beautiful maid's skirt.

With my eyes suddenly opened wide in shock, I looked up at her and whispered, "*WH-what in all fucks?*"

Holding my earlobes tighter, the maid seductively whispered, "Just enjoy it, Mr. Robinson!"

And she let go of my earlobes. She undid her tight skirt and let it drop to the floor. She was wearing no panties, and I was then looking at an erection and a pair of testicles bigger than my own.

"Oh, dear God," I huffed, stuck out my tongue, and began furiously licking and kissing the maid's veiny shaft, not once wondering why I was doing so.

Next, as I kissed and licked her cock (HER COCK?) Teresa began removing her black tight-fitted uniform blouse, revealing the fact that she had no bra on, revealing a pair of big breasts and pointy nipples, beautiful and luscious looking.

Looking upwards, I murmured, "Oh Teresa, you have beautiful tits..." but in response, the maid grinned, said, "Soon, Mr. Robinson, soon..." and guided her cock (HER COCK?) into my mouth.

She began thrusting in and out of my mouth, wiggling her sexy body at the same time.

As I sucked the maid's cock (THE MAID'S COCK?) I continued running my open-palmed hands up and down her black stockinged legs.

For a few seconds, it went through my mind that I was a married guy with kids...and had never cheated on my wife before... AND...I had never sucked a cock before...JESUS!

And just to be clear, I had never sucked a woman's cock before...

Once Teresa's cock (TERESA'S COCK?) was hard as steel, she slid it from my mouth and said, "You seem to like my silk stockings a lot, Mr. Robinson," her huge flagpole (HER HUGE FLAGPOLE?) staring me in the face as she spoke. It was at that moment that I noticed she had no pubic hair.

"Y, yes I do," I murmured as she next stepped out of her high-heeled black pumps, shoes that were most definitely not part of a maid's standard uniform.

As she kicked her pumps aside, the maid slid her cock (HER COCK?) back into my mouth, and as I dutifully sucked that cock, I began rolling her stockings down her legs, something I had always loved doing to women up to and including my wife.

As I slid the maid's stockings down and sucked her cock (HER COCK?) and as her testicles (HER TESTICLES?) crashed into my chin Teresa murmured contentedly, "Feels good, feels so good..." and again reached down to toy with my earlobes. By then, my cock was beyond erect and oozing massive dollops of pre-seed.

When the maid's black stockings were down around her ankles, she again slid her cock (HER COCK?) out of my mouth and balanced herself on one foot at a time to get her stockings off so that we were now both naked as the days we had been born and both of us as stacked up as the Empire State Building at that!

Looking down at me with that hunger still in her eyes, Teresa smiled sexily and said, "Now then, Mr. Robinson, shall we enjoy the bath you drew, or would you rather suck my cock some more and then enjoy the bath you drew?"

Staring up at her in disbelief, feeling total fucking disbelief over this entire encounter, I gobbled her cock (HER COCK?) back into my mouth, began sucking it furiously, and reached around the maid to grip her ass cheeks real tight, kneading those well-shaped ass cheeks of hers as I went on and on sucking her cock... (HER COCK?)

"MMMM..." was the sound Teresa made once again as I sucked her. "I knew you would make this choice, Mr. Robinson. No man can get enough of my cock. No man will admit that, but it is the truth after all."

From what she teasingly said to me, I quickly gathered that I was not the first man Teresa had seduced in this manner, and somehow, I guessed that I wouldn't be the last either.

A few minutes later, five to ten by my best estimates, Teresa and I were seated in the tub of warm, lavender-scented bathwater, facing each other as she now teased my nipples, twisting them, pinching them, driving the tips of her long, sharp fingernails into them. I was grunting and groaning in a mixture of pain and pleasure, something I had never known before...

FUCK THAT, I had never in my life known just how sexually sensitive my nipples were, because, under the water, my erection was churning furiously as this mysterious maid worked her magic on me via my nipples, and my nipples were a part of me that my wife had never explored but I sure as fuck explored hers, *HAR...HAR...HAR...*

When my nipples were as swollen and hard as two pebbles, Teresa, in an amazing show of strength, grabbed my upper arms, hoisted me up in the warm water, and yanked me forward until I landed with her massive erection (HER MASSIVE ERECTION?), this time in my asshole.

"AWWWWWWW, GAWWWWWWWD!" I cried out as her girth (HER GIRTH?) stretched my virgin hole. "AWWWWWW, you sneaky bitch..."

"As I said at the outset of all this, Mr. Robinson, just enjoy it, *just go with it,*" the maid whispered and began riding me up and down on her erect cock. (HER ERECT COCK?)

As Teresa showed astonishing strength, hoisting me up and down on her mammoth-sized girth (HER MAMMOTH-SIZED GIRTH?) invading my rectum every time, she set me down deeper and deeper onto it. I wrapped my muscular arms around her, nuzzled my face into the side of her neck, and whispered, "Oh you bitch, you goddamned mystery from heaven, fuck me, fuck me, *and fuck me hard!* Never before has anyone in my life done this to me!"

And that was exactly what the maid with a cock the size of a python did, ramming into my bowels harder and harder with each thrust.

Under the lavender-scented bathwater, my own cock raged hard and needy, oozing my pre-seed like crazy...

I nipped at Teresa's neck as she held me tighter and rocked me up and down faster and faster on her cock (HER COCK?), the bathwater splashing over the sides of the tub. As the water hit the floor, I stupidly said to myself, "Ah well, no big deal. Teresa is a maid; she'll clean it up."

Fuck, out of all things to be thinking at that moment, there I was, taking a woman's cock (A WOMAN'S COCK?) up my ass, and I was worried about bathwater splashing over the side of the tub.

The maid then, jammed me down hard on her cock, gripped my upper arms super tight, and seethed, "I'm going to cum, Mr. Robinson. I am going to cum now!"

And with that, I felt her warm juices flooding my most private opening, filling my innards, and FUCK, it felt as if my ass was sucking her juices into me.

"AWWWWWWWW GAWWWWD!" I reeled, my voice echoing off the walls of the bathroom. "Now that is an amazing feeling, you sneaky bitch!"

"A dream made flesh..." Teresa whispered in my ear as her load continued sluicing into me.

When she was spent, which felt like an eternity later, I felt her cock slowly deflate inside of me, and I slid off it...

As she leaned her head back and slightly opened her mouth, I didn't need to be told twice what she wanted next.

I stood up in the tub and slid my erection into her mouth, fucking her craw as hard as she had just fucked my damned no longer virgin ass...

"AWWWWW yeah, yeah, you mystery from heaven," I repeated breathlessly as I thrust my manhood into and out of her mouth.

She sucked me hard, licked and kissed the sides of my veiny shaft, reached up, and tugged my testicles as I deep-throated her a few times.

"Gonna feed you my load of executive ball juice," I grunted, pressed my palms against the tile wall, and felt my testicles getting ready to give up their load.

Looking down at Teresa, I could tell she was in ecstasy.

"ARRRRHHHH yeah, FUCKING A!" I ranted then as the maid with a cock tightened her lips around my throbbing erection and gulped down my juices as I began spurting, and she not losing even a drop of me.

When I was spent, Teresa loosened her lip-grip on my cock. I let it slide from her mouth. Breathless, I sat back down in the tub, facing her.

"My God, my fucking God," I said, grinning at the maid. "This would be one for the history books, Teresa, if I weren't a married man that is..."

Smiling back at me, she said, "I'm so glad you enjoyed Mr. Robinson."

That said, she stood up and stepped out of the tub. I watched as she used one of the hotel towels to dry herself off. I lay back in the tub and then watched as she re-dressed herself in her maid's uniform.

"Leaving so soon?" I asked, grinning at her.

"I have to get back to work, Mr. Robinson," she said. "There's so much to do here at the hotel..."

When she was dressed, she picked up my dress socks from the towel rack, held them up, and said, "Souvenir..." and without another word, she left the bathroom...and I heard the door to my hotel room open and then close as well.

"HEH, my socks, a souvenir..." I laughed and picked up a bar of soap to wash with.

Later, when I was dried off, dressed in a pair of white boxer shorts and a black tee shirt, ready for a good night's sleep, the phone on the night table rang. Wondering who would be calling me at this time, I quickly answered it.

"Hello?" I said.

"Hi, Honey, it's me," my wife said.

"Hey, sweetie, how are you doing? Is anything wrong?" I replied.

"No, I just wanted to tell you about the craziest coincidence," she said as I sat down on the bed.

"What coincidence?" I asked.

"Well, you remember my transgender friend, Tony, right?" my wife asked me.

"Of course, the one who always says how much he likes the way I look in my suits and has a thing for the dress socks I wear," I said, grinning and chuckling as I said it, but then my heart started racing because somehow, I knew what my wife was going to say next.

"Tony just called me because he had been out of touch for a while," my wife continued. "He told me he finally had the beginnings of the surgery to transition to female, and, get this, he, well, she, *she* is working as a maid in the hotel you're staying at."

As I heard that the phone nearly fell out of my hand...

"Oh wow, that really is a coincidence," I stammered.

"I agree totally," my wife said. "And she looks beautiful. She just has to have one more surgery, and she'll be one hundred percent female!"

"Yeah, and I bet I know what surgery that is," I said to myself as I felt my asshole still aching.

"Her new name is Teresa," my wife said next, and I flopped back on the bed, a feeling of disbelief filling me. "Anyway, if you happen to see her, please say hello and tell her how great she looks, okay?"

"Sure... sure thing," I said through trembling lips. "I'll even give her a pair of my dress socks as a gift to celebrate her surgery," I added.

At that, we laughed and said goodnight to each other. I hung up the phone and felt my cock engorging in my boxer shorts.

/The End/

Jimmy, the Brutish Construction Worker (Do my dick)

"**Awwwww Yeah, Yeah,** fucking A, do my dick, do my goddamned dick," Jimmy, the thick mustached, robust construction worker, demanded of his train buddy, Christian, as the younger man squeezed, twisted, and stroked the erection that was in the man's jeans. "No one around to see us this early in the wee hours of the morning. AWWWWW, man, fucking fucks, but that feels great, bud. Yeah, do my dick, that's it, do my goddamned dick!" He kept saying.

Grinning like a Cheshire cat, Christian moved his hand down to Jimmy's testicles in his jeans that felt to the young man to be the size of golf balls.

"Damn Jimmy, besides having a thick and lengthy cock, you sure have big nuts as well," Christian muttered as he cupped the construction worker's balls in his hand through the man's jeans and began squeezing and twisting them next.

"All the better to store up my thick and juicy messes of loads," Jimmy grunted. He took a thick cigar from his jacket pocket, wedged it between his lips, and lit it, blowing the smoke in his masturbator's handsome face.

"You know, smoking on a train platform is illegal," Christian said as he went on, squeezing Jimmy's testicles through his jeans.

"Oh yeah? And what you're doing to me IS legal bud?" Jimmy laughed throatily.

After a few more puffs on his cigar, the construction worker took it from his mouth and said, "Nice that you're workin' my nuts, bud, so glad you like 'em and all, but get the fuck back to my dick, do my dick, *do my goddamned dick!*" This time, Jimmy ordered it.

Doing as he was told, Christian quickly let go of Jimmy's balls and once more took the construction worker's erection back in hand, the feel of its steely-like girth through the fabric of the man's jeans magical to the young man.

"AWWWWWWW YEAH, that's it bud, do my dick, do my goddamned dick, your hand and fingers are like magic down there," Jimmy grunted and puffed his cigar.

"I've wanted to do this to you for some time now, Jimmy," Christian said with a grin as he gripped the huge shaft in the man's jeans and ran his thumb round and round the crown of the construction worker's pre cum dripping erection. "Although I never dreamt I would be doing it to you on an early morning deserted train platform, heh..." He added while smiling.

"AW c'mon bud, you said you like danger like I do, so why not do my dick here on a train station platform? YEAH, don't stop, do my dick, do my goddamned dick..." Jimmy panted, puffed his cigar, and blew the smoke in Christian's face. "AWWWW yeah, you do my dick better than the two dudes at my present job site," Jimmy muttered breathlessly now. "Do my dick, man, do my fucking dick..."

"The dudes at your job site?" Christian asked as he kept squeezing and kneading the construction worker's erection of steel through his jeans. "You mean to tell me that you get other guys to do this to you?" Christian looked a little surprised.

"Sure as all fucks bud, I just LOVE the feeling of creaming my mess like this..." Jimmy panted as Christian worked his dick through his jeans even harder now. "...right into my wife's frilly panties that I'm wearing, that I always wear...HA! Imagine that, would you bud? A big dopey macho man like me, wearing his wife's frilly panties and shooting his load in them while another dude or dudes do my dick!"

Christian gripped the man's erection tighter through his jeans, inhaled the cigar smoke blown in his face yet again, and said, "Jesus God that is kinky as all hell, Jimmy..."

"Sure as fuck it is, bud," the construction worker grunted. "FUCK, I'm getting close, Christian. You got good rhythm in that hand and fingers of yours."

"Do your dick, eh?" Christian teased his train buddy.

"Yeah, do my dick, *do my fucking dick*, gonna make a real nice mess of man juice in my wife's frilly panties..." Jimmy seethed.

As Christian went on doing as he was told, he looked into the construction worker's piercing blue eyes and asked, "And what do you do with your wife's cum soaked panties, Jimmy? Do you wear them all through the workday after you've mussed them with your mess?"

"Nah, well, for a bit," Jimmy replied breathlessly now, as his testicles were definitely about to give up their load of man juices. "Usually, they go to the highest bidder."

A smile mixed with a look of total curiosity filled Christian's face as he again had cigar smoke blown in it, while at the same time, he felt the construction worker's erect cock literally churning under his jeans in his wife's frilly panties...

"The highest bidder?" Christian asked as Jimmy began gasping that he was about to cum.

"Y-yeah bud, dudes who do my dick, OOOOOOO fuck, dudes who do my dick get to bid on who gets to keep my wife's cum filled panties as a souvenir," Jimmy grunted, took his cigar from his mouth, slid it between his masturbator's lips, gripped the pole he was leaning against and shot his morning load...into his wife's frilly panties under his jeans. "OOOOOOOOO yeah...feels amazing!

Christian puffed on the cigar as he felt the construction worker's juices flooding his wife's panties and soaking his jeans as well. Obviously, the man didn't give a rat's ass if he rode the train with a wet spot on his jeans' crotch. He was a construction worker after all, and God knew they always had wet spots and other crud on their jeans or work pants.

"AWWWWW man, that was fucking amazing, fucking awesome, thanks bud," Jimmy panted as Christian let go of his cock under his jeans. "Wonder how much I'll get for these panties."

Smiling, Christian puffed the cigar that used to be the now masturbated construction workers', blew the smoke in the guy's face, and said, "I'll give you one hundred dollars. Just tell me where your job site is, and I'll come to collect them at lunchtime."

The two men smiled at each other, and at that moment, other commuters began filling the train platform, all of them unaware of the sexy escapade that had just taken place there.

/The End/

Julian

MY NAME IS JULIAN CORTEZ; I'm a dark-haired, dark-eyed, tall Puerto Rican guy, 38 years old and in great muscular shape. Since I work as the lead singer of a band called "The Hoots" in a nightclub called "The Hacienda" in Astoria Queens, it's imperative that I keep myself in really good physical shape.

Because part of my act is not just singing my lungs out but dancing as well, and the way I dance and swivel my hips while wearing well-fitted suits and ties, I have to say, and not to pat myself on the back, the way I move really gets the ladies in the audience crazy... and it keeps them coming back for more to see me and my band perform. Of course, my wife doesn't really appreciate this part of my act, but hey, like I said, it keeps the ladies coming back and the money rolling into my wallet. I have a family to support, after all.

One night, after a show that lasted an hour and a half, a dude in the audience asked the club manager if it would be possible for him to meet me in my dressing room and get a souvenir of me. I figured the guy simply wanted an autograph. But, what he wanted was beyond my belief...*LOL*!

I was sitting in front of the mirrored table in my personal dressing room in the club, gulping a bottle of cold Poland Spring water, cooling down after all the sweating I had done on stage for the last hour and a half. I had removed my suit jacket and tie and unbuttoned the top two buttons of my white button-down shirt. As I was sitting there, leaning down to unlace my well-polished, shiny patent leather tuxedo-style shoes, I heard the knock on my dressing room door.

"Yeah, come on in," I called out, sitting up in my seat after having unlaced my shoes, not knowing at that moment how unlacing those shoes of mine was fateful that night.

The door opened a bit, and a young guy with blond wavy hair and green eyes stuck his head in the door. I guessed his age to be in the early to mid-20s - definitely a college dude, from what I was able to decipher.

"Mr. Cortez?" the guy asked with a smile.

"That's me," I said. "Come on in."

"Thank you, thank you, Sir," he exclaimed happily, quickly entering my dressing room and closing the door behind him.

I saw that he was dressed in jeans, a pull-over Polo shirt, and loafers...loafers with no socks...I quickly recalled seeing him in the audience and the way he was cheering and clapping and hooting for me after each of my songs was over. I also recalled that he had been sitting with two or three other dudes at his table.

"My name is Travis. Thank you so much for permitting me to come back here and meet you personally," the young man said, holding out a hand as he stepped eagerly over to me.

"It's no problem at all, Travis," I replied and shook hands with him. "I'm always very flattered when someone wants to meet me after a show."

"Yeah, well, you really put on quite a show out there tonight, Mr. Cortez, a regular Ricky Martin you are," he said as I pointed to a chair next to mine, and he sat down.

I smiled and must have blushed three different shades of red before I said, "First of all, Travis, you can call me Julian, and second, I never thought of myself as talented as Ricky Martin."

"Are you kidding, Mr. Cor-er-Julian? The way you dance is better than the way he does," Travis said.

"Well, that is very kind of you to say," I said, opening the top drawer of my dressing table and taking out a journal I always write in after a show. "Now, what can I do for you? I was told you wanted a souvenir of my show, an autograph perhaps?"

"Well, I also wanted to say that the way you dance really makes the bottoms of your suit pants fly up, and since I was seated close to the stage during the show, I couldn't help but notice that you're wearing thick black and thin sheer socks," Travis said and at first I wasn't sure I had heard him correctly.

"UH, yeah, I am wearing sheer socks at that," I said, glancing down at my unlaced shoes. "My wife bought them for me. They're a lot more comfortable than wearing solid black socks, and when my feet sweat in them, they don't bother me as much as regular solid socks..."

As I spoke, I could not believe that I was talking about my damned socks, of all things...I mean, they were just socks, right? *RIGHT?* Well, I would find out very soon that some dudes, like me, for instance, their socks are just that, their socks, but to dudes like Travis, another dude's socks were a whole other story.

"Wow, your wife sure has good taste," Travis said, and I could see that the guy's lips were trembling now as he spoke.

"So, would you like an autograph?" I asked next, taking a pen out of my dressing table drawer.

"Well, that would be really nice, Julian, but I have another, very special request," Travis said, sounding nervous as all hell.

"A, uh, another request?" I asked as the guy was then looking hungrily down at my damned feet. "OH jeez, seriously, Travis?"

"Yes, Julian, please, I would love to have the socks you're wearing as a souvenir," Travis said, sounding so, SO hopeful.

"My socks, you want my socks...*you want my socks?*" I asked incredulously.

"Yes, yes I do," Travis said.

I grinned, crossed one leg over my knee, dangling my unlaced shoed foot, and was unwittingly showing off one of the sheer socks that Travis wanted.

"I got to tell you, Travis, I've had requests for autographs, and I've had requests from women wanting me to sign their thigh, their ass..." I laughed. "But no one, no one has ever requested a pair of my socks as a souvenir of me and my show..."

As my foot dangled, I could see that the guy was practically drooling...

"Uh, Travis, this is more than just a souvenir to you, isn't it?" I asked him.

"You could say that, Julian," Travis said, lifting his head and looking at me. "It would mean so much..."

I pursed my lips, mulled it over for a few seconds, and then said, "Okay, I suppose it couldn't hurt. You need socks, after all. I see you aren't wearing any with your loafers there."

"Oh, I'm not going to wear them, Julian. I would never do that," Travis exclaimed. "I want your essence on them...and wearing them myself would take that essence away..."

Smiling in disbelief, I said, "I can't believe I'm hearing this...but anyway..."

With that, I hefted my right foot up onto my knee and reached for my shoe to take it off my foot so I could get my first sock off for the guy. But as I reached for my shoe, Travis said, "No, no, Julian, *I'll do that for you...*"

The next thing I knew, I had pulled my hand back and was watching as Travis slowly, *so slowly*, slid my shoe off my foot.

"What, what's the point of this Travis?" I asked softly. "I have to say this is all most unusual for me."

"Not to worry, Julian," Travis said, and I nearly blanched when he held the inside of my shoe over his nose and mouth...and DEEPLY inhaled.

"Holy fucks," I whispered.

After he had sniffed and snuffed at my first shoe a bit, he proceeded to reach under my pants leg, his fingers trailing up and over my sheer silk sock slowly...and FUCK of FUCKS, as the guy did his work, I felt my cock bulging up in my suit pants...

When he'd reached the top of my sock, he gripped my calf tightly and whispered, "Calf lengths..."

"Yeah, uh, does that make any difference to you, Travis?" I asked. "I'm really not a tall sock sort of guy, you know?"

"It's fine, Julian, *fine...*" Travis said breathlessly, hooked his fingers and thumb under the top of my sock, and slowly slid it down and off my damned foot.

I have to say there was something weird seeing my naked foot while wearing a suit...

Figuring he would want to get busy with my other foot as soon as possible, I lowered my naked foot to the floor...and then watched in disbelief as Travis held my sock to his nose and mouth and inhaled deeply.

"MMMMMMMMMMM..." was the sound he made as he inhaled my sweaty foot odor from my sock, and I will share that when I dance for as long as I did that night on stage, I really sweat big time, especially on my feet, and I know for a fact just how pungent my socks smell after a show, which is why when I reach home, I instantly put my socks in the washing machine after taking them off because my wife is not crazy about the way my sweaty feet stink up my sheers, but now this guy was sniffing and snuffing my stinky sock like it was the best-smelling thing on God's earth.

When he was done, or when he'd had enough of my first sock, he took a plastic zip-lock bag from his pocket and deposited his prize, my first sock, into the bag.

"Now for the other one, Julian," Travis said expectantly.

"UH, yeah, sure, sure," I replied, lowered my naked foot to the floor, and hefted my other foot up onto my knee.

This time, I simply watched as the guy did his work. He slid my shoe off my foot, held it to his nose and mouth, seemed to inhale the entire odor that was in that shoe, placed it on the floor next to my other shoe, and slid his hand up and under my pants leg once more. This time, when he peeled my sock from my foot I have to admit that my cock was rage hard in my suit pants.

"Thank you, Julian," Travis said as he sniffed my sock a few times, and then he deposited it in the plastic zip-lock along with my first one.

"You're welcome, I guess, Travis," I whispered, my naked foot still resting on my knee.

"If your wife notices that your socks are gone when you get home tonight, what will you tell her?" Travis asked me. "As you said, she bought you the sheers after all..."

"I hadn't given that any thought," I replied, as the guy slid the plastic zip-lock bag containing my sheer socks into his jeans pocket. "I suppose I'll just tell her the truth...if she asks, that is..."

"Yes, if she asks," Travis said softly, leaned in close to me, and kissed me gently on the cheek.

Then, he stood up and looked down at me as I sat there, totally stunned.

"Do you uh, still want my autograph, Travis?" I asked him.

He nodded, patted his pocket where the plastic zip-lock bag that contained my socks was, and said, "I got all the autographs I wanted, Julian. I'll treasure these forever...and look at it this way, if you ever become world famous, I'll be able to say that I have a pair of socks you once wore..."

With that, he leaned down, kissed me again on the cheek, and then he exited my dressing room.

Rubbing the spot on my cheek that he had kissed twice, I whispered, "My God..."

The End

Printed in the United States
by Baker & Taylor Publisher Services